"I'm glad you're a detective. If you weren't, I wouldn't have met you."

He stroked her arm. "Sure you would have. You were mine from the day you were born."

Darlene rimmed her lips with the tip of her tongue, looked at his mouth and then slowly raised her gaze to meet his. "Oh, really?" she said seductively, all the while moving her mouth closer to his. "I never said I was yours."

He pulled her into his arms. "You didn't have to. Actions speak louder than words ever will."

Before she knew it, his hands were all over her while his magic tongue danced in and out of her mouth, giving her a preview of what she was to receive in the moments to follow. She wrapped her arms around the broadness of his body and held on tight.

"Tell me what you want." He stared into her eyes as his fingers teased the flesh of her bare arms, and every place he touched seemed to explode into a blaze. "Tell me."

"I...I want you."

Books by Gwynne Forster

Kimani Romance

Her Secret Life
Forbidden Temptation
Drive Me Wild
Private Lives
Holiday Kisses
Destination Love
Passion's Price

GWYNNE FORSTER

is a national bestselling author of forty-three works of fiction, thirty-four romance novels and nine mainstream novels, including her latest, *When The Sun Goes Down*. She has won numerous awards for fiction writing, including a Gold Pen Award, a *RT Book Reviews* Lifetime Achievement Award, and has been inducted in the *Affaire de Coeur* Hall of Fame. A demographer by profession, she was formerly a senior officer for the United Nations, where she was chief officer in charge of research in fertility and family planning studies. Gwynne is author of twenty-seven publications in demography. She holds a bachelor's and a master's degree in sociology and a master's degree in economics/demography. As an officer, first for United Nations and later for the International Planned Parenthood Federation in London, England, Gwynne has traveled and/or worked in sixty-three countries. She lives in New York with her husband, who is her true soul mate.

Passion's
Price

Gwynne Forster

KIMANI™
ROMANCE

KIMANI PRESS™

ISBN-13: 978-0-373-86200-9

PASSION'S PRICE

Recycling programs
for this product may
not exist in your area.

www.kimanipress.com

Printed in U.S.A.

ACKNOWLEDGMENTS

My sincere thanks to my son (my stepson), Peter Forster Acsadi, who is one of my models for what a man should be. He is an accomplished electronic engineer, and I save my computer and other electronic problems for his attention. A professionally serious, good-natured, witty and handsome man with a laugh that is nothing short of uplifting, he is always there for his parents. With a husband who designs and produces my brochures and answers my panic calls when my software is uncooperative, I enjoy strong family support. I AM BLESSED TO HAVE BOTH OF THEM. As always, I thank God for my talent and for the opportunities to use it.

Chapter 1

When attorney Darlene Cunningham made up her mind, she rarely ever changed it. And that had created some problems for her and her family. As the youngest partner at Myrtle, Coppersmith & Cunningham LLP, Darlene usually got the least promising and least interesting cases assigned in the three-person law firm.

But her job as a defense attorney meant everything to her. Even the smallest detail of the most mundane case got her professional juices flowing. Take for instance her current case. She had to force herself not to get too excited about it. There was something suspicious about her client. Something wasn't right about the burglary case, and it was driving her crazy.

And then a witness had come forward and volunteered to testify on her client's behalf. It all seemed too convenient, she thought. It just didn't add up, and Darlene was determined to find out why.

That's why Darlene had decided to fly down to Memphis and reinterview the witness. Though her partners didn't think it was worthwhile for Darlene to travel all that way just to nail down the facts in the case, Darlene disagreed.

And so here she was in Memphis, trying to locate the alibi witness, the only witness who could testify that her client, Albert Frank, was somewhere else at the time the crime took place. A very convenient witness who had very inconveniently vanished without a trace.

Darlene landed at Memphis International Airport, exhausted after having transferred twice on the trip from Baltimore. Having refused the peanuts and pretzels offered on the plane, she was hungry and a bit on edge. She'd never been to Memphis before, and the intensity of the heat and humidity surprised her, adding to her discomfort.

She checked into the famous Peabody Hotel—known for its duck march through the lobby—and called room service for a pulled-pork sandwich and iced tea. She unpacked while she waited for her food to arrive. After she'd eaten, Darlene once again tried to contact Frank's alibi witness at the number she'd been given. To her disappointment, she got no answer, not even voice mail.

With no word from her witness, she struck out the

next morning to check on her client's story about where the witness lived. She took a cab to the address he'd given her in an upscale neighborhood in a cul-de-sac bordering Memphis and Collerville. She would have expected just about any neighborhood other than the quiet, pristine homes that screamed old-money wealth and power. Less sure of herself now, she knocked on the door, since she had not seen a doorbell.

"Come in," a slender gray-haired man in a black suit, white shirt and black tie said with a gracious smile. "Not many people come here these days." He spoke haltingly, and she decided that he was part of the household staff, a fair assumption given the neighborhood. "Have a seat," the man said as he gestured toward what she discovered was an elegant living room.

"Thank you. This heat is almost unbearable," Darlene said to fill the awkward silence. She used a tissue to wipe her forehead.

"Yes, it is," the man said. "Would you care for some sweetened iced tea? I made it a few minutes ago. If you're uncomfortable, I can turn up the air conditioner."

She leaned against the back of a tufted velvet chair and looked at the man. "Thank you, but I don't care for tea, and the air-conditioning is fine. This is a beautiful house, but it must be very old. No one seems to build these kinds of houses anymore." Small talk was something she hated, but she had to engage the man in conversation if she was to learn anything about her client.

"Yes, it's old, all right. My grandfather built it. But I

renovated it from roof to cellar about twenty-five years ago. Sure you wouldn't like some tea or iced coffee?"

"No thank you. I was given this address and was told a young man, an alibi witness, lived here. But I see I was wrong, so I'd better be going," Darlene said, somewhat surprised that the old man lived in the home. "Thanks for your hospitality."

"I wish you wouldn't go," he said as she reached for the doorknob. "I've enjoyed your company. I don't get much company anymore."

"I'm sorry," she said as she opened the door. She turned to leave, only to find her exit blocked. She looked up into the eyes of a six-foot-three-inch boulder.

"Excuse me. I was j-just leaving," she stammered, taken aback by her sudden encounter with this immovable object.

"You aren't going anywhere," he said.

"Would you please get out of my way," Darlene said, letting him know that she was not easily intimidated.

The man put his hand in the inside pocket of his jacket, took out his badge and flashed it. "I'm Detective Michael Raines of the Memphis Police, and you don't leave this house until I say so."

Darlene looked him in the eye. "Really? I thought all the bullies in uniform were in Baltimore. Apparently Tennessee has some, too. How interesting! Now, would you please move aside? I have business to take care of."

He raised an eyebrow. "Go right ahead. Maybe you can walk through me."

She stared at him, seeing him as if for the first time. Something flickered in his light brown eyes, and she responded, unable to do otherwise. She told herself to get out of there. But she stood rooted to the spot. His eyes said he would never release her. She shook her head as if to break the spell he had cast over her.

"I'm Attorney Darlene Cunningham, and you have no reason to keep me here. If you don't let me pass, I'll sue you, the city of Memphis and the state of Tennessee," she said, her mild manner dissolving into anger.

His facial expression didn't change one bit. Realizing that belligerence would get her nowhere with Detective Raines, she decided to switch tactics.

"You haven't read me my rights, and you have to do that if I'm under arrest." Her voice took on a taunting tone.

"You are not under arrest, Ms. Cunningham. You are being detained."

She leaned her head to the side in what she knew he'd take as a challenge. "What's the difference?" she said, clearly losing patience.

"Very funny, Ms. Cunningham, but you may as well have a seat, because you cannot leave this house until I say so."

Darlene turned to the old man. "You didn't tell me your name."

"My name is Boyd Farmer. Have a seat. At least it's comfortable in here."

"Is this guy your son? Oh, sorry," she said before

Boyd could respond. "You're too nice to have such an arrogant, obnoxious son. I really need to go."

"I'm sorry," Boyd said. "He isn't going to let you go."

She whirled around and glared at Michael Raines, and for her trouble she felt a peculiar thudding in the region of her heart. "At least I deserve to know why I'm being detained," she said. "What did I do?" Realizing that her tone would only make him more adamant, she switched tactics again. "You're unlike any detective I've ever met."

"What do you mean by that?" His tone was definitely not friendly.

"Oh," she said, tossing her hair to the side. "I mean, aren't police officers supposed to protect and serve?"

Boyd's laughter filled the room, but she avoided looking in his direction. Instead she focused on Michael Raines.

"Yeah," he said. "Now, sit down and let's cut the comedy."

Darlene did not like taking orders from a stranger, even one with a badge. She didn't move. "You don't look stupid," she told him. "You have to tell me why you're holding me here. It's the law. Tell me why I'm being detained, or I'm leaving." She tried to move past him.

He grabbed her shoulders and glared at her. "What are you doing here?"

She twisted her shoulders and moved away from him. "I'm trying to get information that I hope will help my client's case."

"You'll have to prove that to me. This house has been under surveillance, and neither you nor anyone else can leave here. Get it?"

She'd have to come up with a different excuse. Getting back to her office in Maryland was paramount. The other partners already considered her trip to Memphis little more than a wild-goose chase, and if they discovered her present predicament… She didn't want to think of their reaction.

"I have to get back to my hotel," she said.

He folded his arms across his broad chest and smiled, giving evidence that he could be charming when it suited him. "Oh, so I gather you plan to leave Memphis."

"No, as a matter of fact I'm staying at the Peabody," she said.

"Really?" he said. "I'm sure it won't be a problem for you to stay here."

"Now, look here, you," she said, with all the softness of a wildcat about to pounce. "You're going to…" She stopped. His beautiful eyes twinkled like flashing lights, and she could see his difficulty in restraining his laughter.

"You're not one bit funny, and I'll have the last laugh."

At that point, Boyd brought the tea along with a brioche and jam. "This should make you comfortable." She thanked him. "Detective Raines doesn't like tea, and I don't have any more coffee," he said.

"How long has he been here?" Darlene asked Boyd, pointing to Michael.

"He's been here two weeks. That's why I don't have any more coffee. He's practically a coffee addict."

She took a few sips of tea and looked at Michael. "Coffee addict, eh? I'm glad to have at least some evidence that you're human."

Something akin to pain flickered in his eyes, and she wished she could retract her words. It wasn't his fault that she'd stumbled into a house that was under surveillance. He was doing his job. Maybe if she appealed to his decency, he'd let her go.

"If I'm stuck here for any length of time, I'll lose my case." She told herself that she wouldn't beg, but that had sounded very much like a plea. She observed him carefully to see his response.

"But how do I know you've told me the truth? You could be the person I've spent the last few weeks looking for."

"Oh, come on," she said, her attitude inching toward aggressiveness again. "Anybody can look at me and see that I'm not a burglar."

He looked toward the ceiling as if begging for mercy. "Another statement like that and I'll have proof that you're not a lawyer."

"I am, and I have to be in court Monday morning. If I don't show up, I'll be in contempt."

"I can take care of that. Give me your client's name and the case number. I'll take care of the problem right now."

"No, thank you. I don't want any help from you."

His quick shrug let her know what he thought of her response.

"You're a heartless man."

"If you say so."

Darlene was already mad with herself. She decided to switch gears one more time, hoping that a different tactic might soften him up. "You ought to be ashamed of yourself for doing this to an innocent person," she chided. "You could ruin my life."

Boyd walked over to where Darlene and Michael stood at loggerheads. "Darlene… I hope you don't mind if I call you Darlene. Wouldn't you like to freshen up a bit? There's a lovely guest room and bath upstairs, and if you're going to be here for a while, you're welcome to use it."

She could see that Boyd wanted to lower the tension between them, so she smiled and patted his arm. "Thanks. That would be lovely."

"Leave your pocketbook and that briefcase down here," Michael said. "And don't think you can use the phone up there. It's been disconnected. On second thought, I'll show you where the guest room is. Who knows what you'll try to do?"

Darlene whirled around and headed for the stairs, intent upon finding the room herself, but he managed to move slightly ahead of her. "This way," he said, turning left at the top of the stairs.

At the bedroom door, she tossed her head back, sending her hair flying around her face.

A grin spread over his face. "Don't even think about

it. That's a thirty-foot drop. You're clever enough to know that if you jumped, you'd hurt yourself. Besides, every window in this house is locked."

Slouched against the doorjamb, Michael stared down at her. Then his gaze shifted from her eyes down to her lips and stayed there. His light brown eyes darkened. His nostrils flared, and he sucked in his breath.

"I don't need you to chaperone me while I go to the bathroom," she challenged.

Not a muscle in his face moved. "Why don't you say what you really mean? Darlene, I could have you thrashing with passion one minute and handcuff you the next."

"I don't believe you," she said, moving toward him.

He folded his arms across his chest. "You're reckless, but I'm not. You're ready to do something stupid right now, and you haven't given a second thought to the consequences."

How many times had she heard those very words from her family? As usual, she ignored the advice. "What consequences?" she asked. "You're a cop, and you're obligated to behave like one."

His laugh was barely more than a groan. "I'm also a man. And since I'm a cop, when it's your word against mine, mine carries more weight. Get in there, wash your face or whatever else you plan to do and stop testing me. If I decide to take you up on your flirtations, you'll remember it for a long time."

"Really? I'd love to know what you'd do."

"What you really want is to *experience* what I'd do to you," he said.

Her jaw dropped. She wasn't used to having anyone be so candid with her. Naturally, she flirted. But it was always harmless. She'd better be careful with this guy, she thought. Still, her mind wondered for a minute if Michael Raines would give her what she'd been missing.

"You're an open book, Darlene, and that makes you dangerous."

She looked at him and said, "Please at least go back downstairs. Your standing here is embarrassing."

"Of course." To her surprise, he headed downstairs.

Almost immediately after Darlene came back downstairs, the doorbell rang. Michael quickly reached the door to open it. He checked the deliveryman's identification, accepted the food and reached into his pocket for his wallet.

"Oh, no, you don't," Darlene said as she rushed to the door and handed the deliveryman a twenty-dollar bill. "Keep the change," she said.

The man looked first at the money and then at Darlene. "It's only eleven bucks, ma'am."

"And I said keep the change," she replied to the astonished deliveryman. He looked at the money again, shook his head from side to side, smiled and left.

Michael did nothing to restrain the grin that spread

over his face. "I don't like you, Detective Raines," she said.

He laughed harder, then looked her in the eye. "That may be the biggest lie you ever told. Say you're irritated or even furious with me, and I'll believe you. But, damn it, you like me. And another thing. Nobody calls me Detective Raines except my mother. If you want a response from me, call me Mike."

"But that's what you said your name is," she told him.

A scowl altered the elegant contours of his face. "It's on my official title, but that doesn't mean I like it. Call me Mike!"

"Since we all have to be here together, can't we be friends?" Boyd asked in his soft, gentle voice.

"That would require civility on all of our parts," Darlene said, mainly to annoy the detective. "I'm not sure that Michael is capable of that."

"Oh, no," Boyd began. "He's always kind to me. If you don't upset him, he's very gentle."

"Thanks, Boyd. You're right," Darlene said. "I've learned that you can calm a rambunctious child by tiptoeing around the little brat."

He knew she was deliberately goading him, and he could give as good as he got, but he'd be damned if he'd let her know that she was getting to him. "I'm surprised that you have any children," he said, disappointed at the possibility that she was married. "It seems a bit too much for you to have gotten a law degree, pursued a career as an attorney, hooked a husband and had children."

From the change in her demeanor, he could see that he had hit a nerve. "What are you suggesting?"

He wasn't sure, but it sounded like she was grinding her teeth. "What's the matter?" He didn't bother to suppress a roguish grin. "In over your head?"

"Michael, I'm twenty-nine. I have two degrees and no children."

He cocked an eyebrow. "Does that mean you've got a man? When does a busybody like you have time for a man?"

He'd upset her with that crack. It was over the line, and he wished he hadn't said it. Her beautiful face seemed to lose its elegance, and even as he looked at her, her dark eyes lost their luster. He wanted to put his arms around her and...

"You're trying to take my mind off the fact that you're unlawfully detaining me." She looked at her watch. "Damn! I should have taken my medicine an hour ago. It's in my hotel room, and if I don't take it soon, I could have a seizure."

He threw up his hands. "Sure, and the Mississippi River runs right through Washington, D.C. I'm not falling for that. Besides, if it were true, you'd carry your medication with you. Try another tactic."

"Aren't you going to eat?" she asked him. "No food, no feelings and no fun?" She grinned. He tried to ignore her. He was trying to protect her, as well as

Boyd Farmer. If she walked out of that house alone, she'd likely walk into trouble.

"Before this is over, you may need my help."

"Let's all try to get along," Boyd said. He looked at Mike, who didn't seem interested. "Oh, by the way, would you please ask your relief to bring a can or two of deep-roasted Columbian coffee and a gallon of milk?"

Mike walked to the window, looked out and turned to Boyd. "I'll bring the coffee and milk when I come tomorrow morning."

Mike noticed Darlene's sudden interest and figured that as soon as his replacement arrived, she'd try to escape.

"Don't even think about it, Darlene. Cody Johnson won't be half as nice to you as I am. If you try to pull a stunt, or even if you give him any lip, he'll take you down to the station and let you cool off in the lockup."

"But I haven't done anything," she said, her big eyes clouding with the threat of tears. Quickly, he turned his back to avoid feeling any sympathy if she began to cry.

"Then I suggest you cooperate."

"Look. I'm tired." She placed the tray that contained the remains of her lunch—hardly touched—on the coffee table and got up. "It's been one long day."

"If you need anything, let me know," Boyd said. "I usually eat dinner around seven, so I'll wake you up about six, and we can order takeout."

"Thanks, Boyd." She reached for her pocketbook.

"That stays right there," Mike said. "Right where I can keep an eye on it."

"Why does knowing my pocketbook is in your care make me unhappy?"

"It's a pity that she has to stay here, Mike," Boyd said. "She's such a lovely young lady."

He couldn't deny that. As she walked up the stairs, the sway of her hips showed Boyd and Mike how a master choreographer perfected a dance. Mike uttered an expletive under his breath.

"Do you think she'll go to sleep?" Boyd asked Mike.

Mike threw up his hands. "Trust me, she won't do anything that sensible. I'll sleep on that sofa over there tonight, in case she tries something foolish."

"I like her," Boyd said.

"What man wouldn't," Mike retorted. "That doesn't mean you can let your guard down. Many a crook has sent a beautiful woman to do his work for him."

Darlene did not have rest in mind. She quietly walked up the stairs, paused at the guest room, turned and looked toward the stairs to see if Mike had followed her. When she saw that he hadn't, she opened and then closed the door to give the impression that she'd gone inside the room. Then she tiptoed down the hall and peeped in what she assumed was the master bedroom, a very masculine setting with a big mahogany sleigh bed, a Bokhara rug and wood blinds. She stepped in, looked in the bathroom and shook her head. No possibility there.

She left the master and looked in the next room. The room next door didn't offer an opportunity for escape, either. Even if she managed to get out, the window was at the front of the house, and she'd be caught.

She saw a door slightly ajar at the end of the hall, peeped in and saw a spa bath. Figuring that if she stepped into the Jacuzzi, she could stand on the edge of it to reach the window, which did not seem to be locked, she decided to risk it. She sat on the edge of the treadmill, pulled off her four-inch heels and stepped into the tub. After an exhausting struggle balancing precariously on the edge of the Jacuzzi, she managed to raise the window about eight inches. She grabbed the windowsill, pushed her body upward, closed her eyes and got as much as her shoulders out of the window.

"What the hell do you think you're doing, woman? Are you trying to kill yourself? Not even a fool would deliberately plunge headfirst into a rock garden!"

She didn't realize that her skirt hem had crawled nearly to her waist until she felt his strong fingers clasp her thighs. As scared as she was, the feeling of his hands, gentle but firm, sent shock waves through her body. With one hand just below her buttocks and the other under her armpits, he pulled her body inch by inch back into the room.

"This window won't open any farther," he said, "and I don't want to hurt you. Try to move your head to the side so that I can get you in here without bruising you."

"Nobody asked you to do this," she said, fuming at having been caught. "Take your hands off me."

"Now you listen to me, Darlene. If you'd been successful, you'd be dead by now. Jumping feetfirst would have rewarded you with a broken leg and maybe a severely injured spine, but headfirst…" He pulled her in a bit more. "I've tried to protect you, but you don't believe you're in jeopardy. If I open that front door and give you permission to leave, I guarantee that you wouldn't reach the end of this block without being followed. If you were lucky enough to get to your hotel, you'd be a sitting duck there."

"Nobody would bother me in that hotel."

His left hand cradled the back of her head as he eased her feet to the bottom of the Jacuzzi.

"Don't ever do anything like that again," he said, still holding her in his arms.

Embarrassed, frustrated and flustered, intending to give him one of her razor-sharp barbs, she looked up at him and gasped. Every inch of her skin, every nerve in her body responded to the fiery turbulence in his eyes. She couldn't move and didn't want to.

"You…uh…you can put me down now."

With his hand at the back of her head, he stared down into her eyes. "That isn't what you want, and it is definitely not what I want." His lips were an inch from hers.

"Open your mouth and take me in."

"P-put m-me down. I…" His lips parted, and his masculine aura enveloped her until, nearly out of her mind with a strange, peculiar need for him, her hands went behind his head and brought his mouth to hers.

"Kiss me, baby." The hoarseness of his voice communicated a sense of urgency. She pulled him into her mouth and tasted him as if she'd never had anything so good. His tongue began to dip and sample every crevice of her mouth, teasing and tantalizing her until the heat at her core made her thighs tremble. He didn't spare her, and when his hand went to her breast, she clasped the back of it, pressing it to her flesh. He rubbed her nipple until she was ready to beg him to take it into his mouth. But when his other hand went to her buttocks, she came to herself and moved back. He released her at once.

But he brought her back to him in a gentle hug that heightened her desire. "You didn't intend for it to go that far, and neither did I, but don't tell me you're sorry."

"I'm not in the habit of lying, Detective—I mean Mike."

"So you're not sorry?"

She stepped out of his embrace and put on her shoes. "A lot of good being sorry would do. I just want to get back home."

He began to readjust his clothing, revealing taut muscular abs. He was the epitome of the kind of man she'd dreamed of.

"Some people kiss and tell. It seems you kiss and run."

Without thinking, she threw her left shoe at him. "You know exactly how to get on my last nerve."

"I don't get on your nerves, Darlene. I remind you that you're a woman, and you don't want to think about that." He picked up the shoe and handed it to her.

Darlene jumped up. With her body inches from his, she wagged her finger in his face. "If you say something like that to me again, I'll…I'll…"

He grabbed the moving finger. "You'll what? Come, let's go downstairs. Boyd probably thinks I've killed you."

"You're probably right," she said. "I suspect he's not dealing with a full deck, but he's such a sweet man. I like him."

He took her hand and then dropped it. "Yeah. I like him, too. A lot, and as long as I have this job, nobody's going to harm him."

A frown creased her face. Did Mike think her capable of harming Boyd, or anyone else? She left his side and rushed down the stairs ahead of him, annoyed with herself for having what, until that moment, had been for her a tender, sweet and memorable kiss.

He bounded down the stairs behind Darlene and stepped in front of her. "What tripped your trigger this time?"

With a toss of her head, she walked around him. "You do that more easily than anybody I ever knew."

"I don't doubt it. Let me know when you figure out why."

"Are you all right, Darlene?" Boyd asked her. "What happened? I don't think you had time to get a little rest."

"No, I didn't. But Michael, I mean Mike, wanted to be certain that I stayed in line, so he came up to check on me. I think I'll stay down here so that he can keep an eye on me."

"She means I caught her trying to escape out of the window. Tonight, she sleeps down here on the couch."

"Oh, my," Boyd said. "I do wish the two of you would be friends."

"Thanks, Boyd, but try being friends with an angry lion and see where you end up. I should be allowed to make a call."

"Stop worrying. I called your brother Clark, and he said you're getting precisely what you deserve, because you're nosy and you're always getting into things that aren't your business."

She glared at him. "You telephoned my brother? How'd you find him, and who told you I have a brother?"

Mike lifted his right shoulder in a quick and dismissive shrug. "It appears that the Cunninghams of Frederick, Maryland, are well-known. I'm a police detective. There isn't much I can't find out."

"I could dislike you a lot."

She wanted to wipe the smug expression off his face.

"But you won't. You're a smart lawyer, and that means you have a good memory. I'm betting you won't be able to forget what happened upstairs for a long time."

She opened her mouth to deny it, but she was a good lawyer, and she couldn't lie. Without saying a word, she sat down and looked away from him.

Chapter 2

The doorbell rang. Mike started toward the front door, stopped and turned to Darlene. "Stay put and don't say a word. It could be anybody, and you could be in danger." He put his right hand under the left side of his jacket and went to the door.

"Hey, man, am I glad to see you," he said after slipping the chain and opening the door. "I need to pick up a few things. There isn't a bit of coffee in this house."

Mike led another man into the room.

"You can bring some when you come tomorrow morning," the other man said.

"I'm thinking of changing things here. You have a family, and I don't. This is a four-bedroom house, so I can bunk here," Mike said as he led the other man, presumably his replacement, into the living room. "Come on in, and I'll introduce you to the latest addition to our problem. Detective Cody Johnson, this is attorney Darlene Cunningham." Cody walked over to Darlene and looked at her, though he didn't offer to shake hands.

"How'd you get involved in this?"

"I rang the doorbell, Boyd let me in and his honor over there detained me. I'm grateful that I'm not in handcuffs."

"I see you're full of attitude. You've got a mouth on you, too." Cody turned to Mike. "How'd she get past you?"

"That's one of the things that's bothering me, Cody. A green Jaguar cruised slowly past here three times yesterday. This morning, it came by again, slowing almost to a crawl when it passed this house, so I followed it until it turned into Route 61 and headed toward Mississippi. That took me away for about fifteen minutes. When I got back here, Ms. Cunningham was about to leave. I'm not certain that her arrival at precisely that time wasn't planned."

Cody rubbed his chin with his right thumb and index finger. "I see." He walked over to Boyd. "How's it going, man?"

"Wonderful, Cody. Darlene is a lovely woman and so pleasant."

"I guess you or any other man would say that after weeks of only Mike and me for company."

Cody Johnson had spent a quarter of a century in the Memphis police force. He'd worked his way up to the job of detective, which he'd held for the past six years. At fifty years of age, he was a hardened lawman, though fair and honest. He walked back to Darlene. "Detective Raines is in charge of this operation, but when it comes to dealing with criminals, I take a backseat to no man. So, if you haven't committed a crime, be sure to maintain that record on my watch. If you do, I'll handcuff you and take you to jail."

"What kind of crime can I commit with you watching my every move?"

"Resisting an officer is a crime."

"I'm a practicing attorney. Thanks for educating me."

Mike watched the interplay between Darlene and Cody and concluded that Darlene wouldn't last five hours in the house with Cody. She couldn't resist being a smartass, and Cody wouldn't tolerate it.

"I'll go home, pack a bag and pick up some food for Boyd. I should be back here in about two and a half hours. So call Gail and tell her you'll be home for dinner."

"Works for me, man. I'd hate to have to arrest Ms. Cunningham, but with her mouth, she'll be in that jail on Haley Road before it gets dark," Cody said.

Mike walked over to Boyd. "Since I'm going to the supermarket for coffee and milk, what else do you need?

"Thanks for asking, Mike. We need bread, some

more brioche, butter and…" He looked at Darlene. "What do you like to eat for breakfast?"

"I'll eat whatever you have, but I love any kind of berries, scrambled eggs, bacon and toast."

Boyd looked at Mike.

"Okay. Okay. I get the message," Mike said. "See you later." He headed to the door. Then, as in an afterthought, he went back to Darlene. "Darlene, please obey Detective Johnson. I wouldn't want you to spend a night in a Shelby County jail. But if he takes you there, I'll know you deserved it."

He didn't feel any better for having warned her again, since he knew that being a smartmouth was as much a part of her as breathing. He knew he'd better get back there in a hurry.

He could have released her at once, and perhaps he should have, because he didn't believe she knew anything about the case involving Boyd. But she went there seeking information—according to her—and hadn't told him what she was looking for or why. He'd acted according to the law, and he wouldn't allow his physical attraction to her to lure him into doubting his professional judgment.

He put his key into the door of his apartment, but the door opened before he could open it. "Mr. Raines, I didn't know you'd be here this evening," Jessie, his housekeeper, said. "This whole place is torn up. The carpets, bedding and cushions have to be aired out and cleaned every so often. Ain't no place for you to sit down."

He patted her shoulder. "Not to worry. I'm on stakeout tonight and for how long I don't know, maybe two nights, maybe a month."

She put her hands on her hips and looked up at him. "You be careful now. You hear?"

"I'll do that, Jessie. What kind of coffee do you buy for me?"

"Any deep-roasted Columbian coffee is good." She wrote down the brand that she bought and handed him the note. "I think this is the best around here."

"Thanks." He went to his room, packed what he'd need for three days and came back to the den, where Jessie was polishing furniture. "You have my private number in case you need me. I'll be in touch."

"Yes, sir. I sure hope it's air-conditioned where you gonna be."

"I'll be comfortable. See you." After he got behind the wheel of his silvery gray SUV, he wished he'd remembered to ask Jessie which supermarket she usually went to. He stopped at the first big supermarket he saw, bought the items on his list along with two six-packs of beer, two bags of Cajun-style corn chips and a bag of his favorite candy bars.

"If I'm gonna be held hostage by temptation, I may as well have something to divert my attention," he said aloud while storing his purchases in the trunk of his car.

* * *

"That was pretty fast," Cody said when Mike returned after less than two hours.

"Stay for a cup of coffee, Cody. Mike makes wonderful coffee," Boyd said. He looked at Mike. "I hope you remembered what Darlene likes for breakfast."

He didn't like being put on the spot in Cody's presence, so he shrugged to give the appearance of disinterest. "I bought what you asked me to buy."

"Good," Boyd said. "Will you make us some coffee?"

Mike wondered, not for the first time, if Boyd was really mentally challenged or very shrewd. He could tell Boyd to make the coffee himself, but he'd hate the taste of it. "Sure. As soon as I put this stuff away," he said. He quickly stored his stuff in one of the spare bedrooms, then made the coffee. Boyd relieved him of the job of serving it.

"If I have to have police protection, I hope Mike stays with me, because he is such a kind and considerate gentleman," Boyd said to Darlene.

Cody cleared his throat. "Yeah, he is *that,* provided you don't break the law or otherwise get on the wrong side of him."

Mike knew Darlene was deliberately refusing to look at him. What had happened to her rambunctious behavior? Was this show purely for Cody's benefit? Mike wondered if Darlene the hellion would reappear the moment his partner walked out the door.

"This is really good coffee," Darlene said to Mike, interrupting his thoughts.

"Thanks. All I did was put coffee in the filter, put it over a coffeepot and pour boiling water over it. No sweat involved."

"It's good," she said, looking at Boyd.

Just then, Cody emptied his cup and stood. "Good stuff, man. If you need me, you have my number."

"Is he coming back?" Darlene asked Mike.

"Not tonight. I'll be here tonight." He looked at Boyd. "We've decided to stay inside for a while, instead of outside in the car. If the people who are after you don't see one of us sitting out there, they may decide to show their hand.

"Nothing's stopping them now. They could walk in just as Darlene did," Boyd responded. "By the way, won't they see your car out there? They'll know you're still here, won't they?"

"I changed cars. They won't recognize this one." He looked at his watch. "It's six twenty-five. Why don't we watch the evening news?"

"When do we eat dinner?" Darlene asked them. "I'm getting hungry."

"I guess you are," Mike retorted. "You barely touched that stuff you ordered for lunch. Are you on a diet?"

She shook her head. "No, I'm not."

"And you're not taking any medicine, either?" When she shook her head, he became concerned. "I suspected that." He softened his voice so as not to annoy her. "You seem subdued, and I'm not sure I like that. You're a fighter. What happened while I was gone?"

"I'm tired," she said, but he didn't believe her. He went into the kitchen, ostensibly for more coffee, and called Boyd in for a private conference. "Did Cody and Darlene have a problem while I was gone?"

"Well, she managed to tell him that she didn't like cops, and he told her he wasn't going to babysit a smart-mouthed woman and that if she said anything else to him, she'd be in jail before you got back here. Then he took out the handcuffs and put them on the coffee table. I think she got the message."

Mike couldn't help feeling her pain, but he knew that, if pushed, he would do the same. He poured a second mug of coffee, added milk and took it to her.

She looked up at him, and smiled. "Thanks so much. I wanted some, but I didn't feel that I should ask."

In other words, the weight of her predicament had settled on her. "I hope this will soon be over, Darlene, and you can get on with your life."

"There was no way that I could have avoided this, Mike. I need to verify my client's alibi if I'm going to clear him. The information I have led me here. What was I supposed to do but come here?"

"I always check things out first. You should have done that *before* you came to Memphis. Develop a good relationship with a first-class detective and talk to him or her. Investigations require special training and experience, without which you can walk right into a trap."

"I don't know any detectives in Frederick."

"There must be someone in Baltimore. This business is too dangerous for a neophyte."

He saw that she took in every word he'd said and told himself to back off. Her safety was not his concern. In truth, he shouldn't have cared whether she was in danger or not. But he might as well admit it: *he didn't want anything to happen to her,* he thought to himself.

"Thanks, Mike," she said. "I'm the youngest in a three-person firm. How can anyone develop professionally in that environment? I work there, because being a partner in the firm is worth ten times the experience I'd get as a lawyer working alone.

For some reason he had an overwhelming desire to protect Darlene, but that wasn't his job. He was there to protect Boyd. "I suggest we order dinner. It'll be nearly an hour before it arrives." He looked at Darlene and winked. "I take it you don't want what you had for lunch."

He could see that she bristled. "Don't remind me of that. I want a soup and salad."

"Okay," Mike said.

"What are you having?" Darlene asked Mike.

So she wanted to be friendly. Fine with him. "Probably a burger and fries."

"I'll have what Mike's having," Boyd said.

Mike paid careful attention to Boyd. He wanted to make sure Boyd, who was a witness in a high-profile drug case and in protective custody, made it to trial.

* * *

Darlene had realized that Cody Johnson wasn't as accommodating as Detective Raines. She had prayed that Mike would soon return. She decided to refrain from annoying Mike so that he wouldn't call in a replacement.

"Do you mind if I go to the bathroom and freshen up?" she asked Mike. "I wish I could change. I'm sick of these clothes."

"You'll find a white terry-cloth robe in the guest-room closet," Boyd said. "Why don't you take off your shoes and let your feet rest? You won't mind, will you, Mike?"

"Check out the guest room," Mike said to Darlene. "You might be surprised by what you find?"

She slowly went up the stairs, suspicious that Mike didn't follow her. In the guest-room closet, she found the terry-cloth robe and a pair of white furry slippers. Unfortunately, they were too small for her feet. In the bathroom, which was painted and tiled in gray, she found the makings of a luxurious bath. She wrapped her hair in a towel, filled the tub, sprinkled the bath salts in the water and stepped in. Enormous bubbles covered her body, and she closed her eyes as the scent of one of her favorite perfumes filled the room. Within minutes, she fantasized that Mike Raines's strong fingers were stroking her legs. Then they moved boldly to her thighs. She parted them, and his fingers went into her, gently massaging her. She wet her lips and a moan escaped her lips, bringing her to her senses.

"My Lord!" she exclaimed aloud. "Have I lost my mind?"

She got out of the tub, dried off, washed her face and dried it with a plush gray towel. She examined the silver hairbrush on the dressing-room table, decided that it was clean and its bristles strong. She tamed her hair with it, then dressed again in the clothes she had been wearing earlier. She started down the stairs and saw Mike coming up.

"It hasn't been forty minutes," she said when they stood side-by-side on the same step.

""I know that."

"Don't you trust me?"

"Oddly enough, I do."

"Then—"

Without a word he pulled her closer and bent toward her lips. Still hot from her lovemaking fantasy, tremors shot through her and her breath caught short. When she wet her lips, he picked her up and carried her back to the guest room and closed the door.

"This doesn't make a bit of sense to me, Darlene, but I want you."

"I hoped that you'd come back. I don't know what I'd have done if it had been someone else for the rest of the stakeout."

"Because of Cody?"

"No. Because I wanted you. I can still feel your hands on my body easing me through that window. I can—"

His tongue slid along the seams of her lips and frolicked there for a second before she opened her mouth and sucked him in. He tasted and tested every crevice and every centimeter of her mouth, until she felt the warmth ease down her leg as she undulated her body against him. He pulled her closer, and she feasted on him as more heat plowed through her. She rocked against him. Frantic for more of him, she grabbed his hand and rubbed it against her aching nipple. Mike plunged his hand into the neckline of her blouse and tortured her nipple. When she moaned aloud, he lifted her, braced himself against the doorjamb and sucked her nipple into his greedy mouth. She held his head to her and let him feast until the feel of his arousal brought her to her senses.

She pushed against his chest. "Oh, no. I'm sorry, Mike. I didn't mean for this to happen, but I was still… I mean I'd been thinking… Oh, I don't know what I mean."

He set her on her feet, adjusted her blouse and caressed her cheek.

"I can't believe I went crazy like that, Mike. I've never in my whole life felt like that. I'm—"

"When were you thinking of me? Just before you met me on the steps," he whispered.

She could lie or she could get mad at him. She did neither. "A few minutes before you met me on the stairs. How did you know?"

"Because your face blushed with color, and you wouldn't look me in the eye. What do you mean you never felt that way before?"

"I haven't."

"I see. Is there a man in your life now?"

She buried her face in the curve of his neck. "No one."

"There's a strong physical attraction between us, Darlene, and I think we ought to see where it takes us. What about it?"

"I don't know. I live in Maryland, and you're here. Besides, I'm not sure I want a guy who can make me do what I just did."

He stepped back and stared at her. "I hope you're kidding. You want to be with a man who can't fire your passion? That makes no sense to me."

"Come on," she said. "Let's go downstairs before Boyd decides we're up to something. Besides, won't he sneak out?"

"No. He's afraid to do that. You never answered my question."

"But we don't know each other, Mike."

"Right. And I'm asking that you give us a chance to get to know each other. I want to know what makes you happy, what ticks you off, angers you, saddens you, your hobbies, your joys, secrets, likes and dislikes. Are you a Republican or a Democrat?"

"Don't insult me by even suggesting that I could be a Republican."

"At least I know that much." He put an arm around her. "Our food should be here any minute. Come on."

He paid for the food, and she neither objected nor questioned him about it. The three of them ate before sitting down to watch a movie. At about nine o'clock, Boyd announced that he was going to bed.

"You take the guest room, Darlene, and Mike—" said Boyd.

"I'm sleeping down here on the sofa."

"Sure," Boyd said. "The sofa opens into a double bed. See you tomorrow morning. Good night, Darlene. I'm sorry you have to be here, but in a way, I'm glad you came. You brighten the place."

Darlene watched as he climbed the stairs—almost jauntily, she thought.

"He seems happy," Darlene said to Mike when they were alone.

"I think he is. He likes you a lot. You're gracious and…well, gentle with him."

"So are you."

"I'm just being myself. A woman expresses gentleness quite differently than a man. Besides, he doesn't want me fussing over him, but your little pats on his arms and his shoulders make him feel cherished."

She walked over to Mike and gave his shoulder a soft caress. "Did that make you feel cherished?"

His eyes darkened, and his nostrils flared. "Unless you want to spend the night on this sofa with me, get up those stairs."

She cocked her head to the side and exhaled deeply. "Nobody orders me around, Mike. I'll go up the stairs when I get ready."

"If you're trying to see what I'm made of, you're

moving in the right direction. I want to make love to you, and if you don't get up those stairs now, I will."

"Don't be so sure."

"I know the music that makes you dance, and I'm skilled at playing it." He walked toward her, but she stepped backward until her back touched the arm of the sofa. The next minute she was lying on her back, and he was standing over her. "What will it be, Darlene? This isn't a time for teasing."

She raised her right hand to him. "Please help me up. I want to kiss you good-night, but I'm scared to."

He helped her up and wrapped her in his arms, but before she could return the caress, he pressed a quick kiss to her lips and released her. "Sleep well, baby. By the way, I forgot to give you this travel-size toiletry pack. I bought it at the supermarket."

Her arms went around him. "You're so sweet. It's just what I needed. Thanks."

"You're welcome," he said, his voice rough and shaky. "Now, go on upstairs."

She parted her lips over his and took his tongue into her mouth. "Night." She ran up the stairs. He didn't know it, but, as mad as he made her sometimes, she didn't see herself ever forgetting about him.

Mike opened the sofa bed and smiled. He had expected to have a miserable night's sleep on a sofa with his feet hanging off it, but the large mattress guaranteed comfort. He took a shower and headed back downstairs as quickly as possible, carefully avoiding the room in which Darlene slept. For whatever reason the woman was temptation personified. But not even the thoughts of her soft and willing body tight in his arms was going to make him violate his official oath—to serve and protect. Bad enough that he'd kissed her while on duty, but he was not going further than that.

He checked the front and back doors, turned off the lights and slipped between the sheets, irritated that for modesty's sake, and in the event of an emergency, he had to sleep in pajama bottoms. He loved the feel of his naked flesh against cool, clean sheets. He closed his eyes and told himself to sleep—a routine that usually guaranteed he'd doze off quickly. But instead of sleeping, he spent the next two hours tossing and turning, half-awake. Exhausted, he sat up and turned on a light. He knew the symptoms had to do with Darlene and his sexual frustration. What had caused him to think such a thing? After drinking a glass of warm milk, he got back in bed and was soon asleep.

He awakened, groggy and tired. "Wake up, Mike. I brought you a cup of coffee," Boyd said. "It's not as good as yours, but it will wake you up."

"Thanks, Boyd. What time is it?"

"Seven-thirty, and I just heard Darlene upstairs, so you'd better get dressed."

He sipped the coffee. "You're improving. This is good." He got up, dressed, made the bed, closed the sofa bed and drank the remainder of the coffee. What had Boyd Farmer been like before his life was turned upside down by the witness protection program? The question had begun to bother him. Boyd was no different than any other person minding their own business only to have their life turned upside down after witnessing a murder. After washing up, Mike walked into the kitchen, where Boyd stood peeling a pineapple.

"Mind if I ask you a question or two, Boyd?"

"Nope. I may not answer, though," he replied, continuing to cut the fruit.

"Who are your close relatives—for example, people you would want to be contacted if you got sick?"

Boyd stopped peeling the pineapple and looked directly at Mike. "I have two nieces, a nephew and a cousin, and I don't want any of those vultures near me."

Mike's mouth dropped. "*What?* But—"

"Surprised you, didn't I?"

"Absolutely. You mean if you died, you wouldn't want your relatives to know?"

"Right. They wouldn't care. Do you know how to make pancakes?"

"Yeah. I take 'em out of the box and pop 'em in a toaster."

He hadn't heard Boyd laugh before, and the sound of it surprised him. "I was hoping for some homemade."

"I wondered where you two were. Good morning," Darlene said.

"Good morning," Mike responded. "Did you sleep well?"

"You bet I did. That bed is pure luxury. How'd you sleep down here?"

I fought the sheets half the night trying to deal with my passion for you, he said to himself. "Fine," he said, and made himself grin.

"Have you ever made pancakes, Darlene?" Boyd asked. "I'd love to have some."

Darlene rolled up the sleeves of her blouse. "Give me flour, baking powder, eggs, milk, salt, butter and fifteen minutes."

Mike stared at her. "I wouldn't have thought you could boil water."

"I've been known to burn it," she shot back. "Boyd, do you have any maple syrup?"

"Oh, yes. I'll fry some bacon."

Darlene looked at Mike, her eyes sparkling with mischief. "Think you can set the table, Detective Raines?"

"Yes, ma'am."

Half an hour later, the three of them sat down to a breakfast of fresh pineapple, pancakes and bacon. "These pancakes are delicious," Mike said.

"Oh, yes. They're real good," Boyd said. "I hate not going out, but having company for breakfast and dinner is better than going out by myself."

Mike glanced at Boyd in time to see Darlene stroke his arm in a gesture of comfort. He could use some of that himself.

A loud crash interrupted this thoughts. He pushed away from the table. "Get under the table, both of you," he said. He grabbed his revolver and ran to the hallway that led to the rear of the house. The sound came from the direction of the back of the house. The shattered windowpane told him that he'd guessed right. He unlocked the door and stepped outside just as a man attempted to scale the high fence and escape.

"Drop or I'll shoot! *I said drop!*" The man fell to the ground. "And don't move an inch."

"My leg hurts."

"Too bad. Get up, face that wall and don't turn around unless you want a bullet." He dialed the detective's squad room. "This is Raines. I caught a guy scaling the wall after he tried to break in the back door at Boyd's place." He dialed Boyd's number.

"Hello."

"Boyd, this is Mike. I'm holding a guy out back here. If two policemen come to the door, let them in and show them the way to the back of the house."

"Okay, but you be careful."

"I've got it covered, Boyd."

Within ten minutes, Cody Johnson and another officer arrived. "Good work, Mike," Cody said. "We'll take him off your hands."

"But I have to file my report, so—"

"You've been up all night, man. It can wait until tomorrow. Breaking and entering will get him a nice rest, so one extra day won't matter," Cody said. "By the way, please give my regards to Miss Hellraiser."

Although he winced at the dig about Darlene, Mike forced a grin. "I'll do that. Thanks, buddy."

* * *

Darlene held Boyd's hand. "Don't worry," she said. "Whatever it is, I know Mike can take care of it."

"You're right," Boyd said. "Ever since I met him, I wished I'd had a son like him." He cleared his throat. "Darlene, I think I ought to tell you something. You've been so nice to me that I feel badly for not having been straight with you. I haven't been straight with Mike, either."

"What is it?" she asked cautiously.

"I'm under house arrest until I testify in a big case. That's why I appreciate Detective Raines," he said. "But after I testify I'm on my own or it's the witness protection program."

"What will you do?"

"I don't know. I think that's what's behind these attempted break-ins. Pretty soon, Mike's going to release you, but I want you to stay in touch and come visit me. I never married, so I don't have any children. You'll always be welcome here." He was quiet for a moment. "You and Mike, work things out. He's a good man, and you won't find one like him every day. Do you hear me?"

"Yes, I hear you, and I'm sure that you're going to be all right. Thank you for everything, Boyd."

"Something serious seems to be developing between you two. Don't ignore it."

They both walked to the front of the house. Darlene followed Boyd to the front door. "Detective Johnson, what's happened? Is Mike...Detective Raines all right?"

"You bet. We came to arrest the intruder."

She let out a long sigh. "Thank God." Cody regarded her suspiciously, wondering if anything was going on between his partner and her. Even so, it could have been that she was relieved nothing serious had happened to Mike.

"Come with me," Boyd said. At that, Cody's eyebrows shot up, and he looked around as if assuring himself that he was in the right place. Boyd was not behaving like a man who was under house arrest.

Darlene followed them down the hall to the door that led to the rock garden, stepped outside and satisfied herself that Mike was indeed safe. Later, after Cody and his partner left with the assailant, Mike sat down with Darlene and Boyd.

"The officers at the station will be arraigning the suspect, Darlene, and if they can detain him, you'll be free to leave. Until then, I'm still on duty here. However, if you or Boyd would like to get some fresh air in the garden back here, I'll be glad to go with you. I think he's the guy I've seen driving past here, but I want to wait for the police report."

"Let's order some lunch," Boyd said. "By the time it gets here, I'll be hungry." Once it was delivered, the three of them sat on benches in the rock garden enjoying the fountains and the birds that came to use the birdbath. After a while, Boyd decided to go into the house to get some bird feed.

"I guess this the end for us, Darlene. I was hoping that somehow you'd stay a little longer. I want a chance to *know* you and to show you who I am. Though since I've met you, I'm no longer certain that I know myself."

She stroked the back of his hand. "I guess the biggest surprise has been my reaction to you, Mike."

He took both of her hands. "Don't you want to get to know me?"

"Yes, but you scare me, because I don't know what you'll do."

"If you're talking about the Mike who kissed you last night, trust me, the better you get to know him, the happier you'll be…that is, if I'm the guy who teaches you."

"But what about the distance between Maryland and Memphis?"

"If the planes don't fly, I can always drive. If you tell me I can see you, believe me, I'll be there."

"Why, Mike? We hardly know each other."

"Darlene, this is something you should know about a man and a woman—it only takes a moment. For me, that moment was when I opened that door as you were about to leave." He stared hard at her.

Chapter 3

Darlene had hoped that Mike would not receive the call from the police station for at least another day. But shortly after lunch—about three hours after Mike had apprehended the suspect—Mike got the news that the man would be arraigned and that he no longer needed to detain Darlene.

"You're free to leave here whenever you like, Darlene," Mike told her. She sat still, looking at him, unaware of the disheartened expression on her face. "You don't seem happy about the prospect of leaving," Mike said. "If you'd like, I'll drive you to the Peabody Hotel." There was an officer outside who would continue to watch Boyd.

"I've been in another world for two days," she said,

"and I realize now that it's been pleasant and I…I feel as if I'm leaving friends."

Mike narrowed his eyes, spread his knees and clasped them with the palms of his hands. "Friends, eh?"

Neither of them was prepared for Boyd's laughter. "That's what I was thinking," he said.

Darlene got up and walked toward Boyd, who stood as she approached. "I don't have anything to pack," she said to no one in particular. She smiled and hugged the older man. "I'm glad I met you. I wouldn't have missed knowing you for anything." She kissed his cheek. "Before I leave Memphis, I'll be in touch." Then she picked up her handbag and turned to Mike. "I'm ready."

Once they were settled, he started the car, turned on the air-conditioning and pulled away from the curb. "I don't feel like driving you to the hotel and leaving you there," he said.

She hadn't thought that Mike would feel anxious about her leaving, or that he would feel as uneasy as she felt. *I've learned more about myself in the past two days than in the past ten years,* she thought to herself. "I told you that I'll stay in touch, Mike. If it's at all humanly possible, I keep my word," she said. She could almost feel him relax.

"When are you returning to Maryland, and what will you do for the remainder of your stay?"

"After I look over my notes, I'm going to get the information that I came here to get, and I hope that won't take more than an additional day."

"Be careful. If I can help, let me know."

He stopped the car in front of the hotel and put his official police ID against the windshield. He wrote something on the back of his card and handed it to her. "Don't lose that. For obvious reasons, my phone number is unlisted." He got out of the car and went around to open her door. "I know it's old-fashioned, but I like to open doors for women when they're special to me," he said.

"How many women are special to you?"

He tweaked her nose. "You are. I'll walk you to your room."

She appreciated his courtesy, but she also wanted to work. And she didn't think that she would accomplish much if he were in her room with her.

At the desk, she asked for another room key and got a knowing look from the desk clerk, who handed her the card key along with a handful of messages. Once they reached her door, she tried to avoid looking at him.

"Why can't you look at me?" he asked, as he closed the door behind them.

She looked up at him and breathed deeply. She didn't see the fiery passion that had burned in his eyes the night before, but rather a tenderness, a sweetness that she had never before seen in any man's eyes. She automatically moved toward him and welcomed the loving warmth of his arms around her and the feel of his hands on her body.

"Darlene, I'd like to have dinner with you tonight," he whispered, hugging her.

"You've practically guaranteed that I'll say yes. I'm no match for you."

He moved back an inch and stared into her face until her blood began to warm her veins in a mad race to her loins. As if he read her reaction to him, he brushed her lips with his, and she opened to him. Then he plundered her lips and possessed her until her body slumped against him.

"If I don't get out of here… I'll never be able to leave." He kissed her quickly and left without waiting for her response. Shaken, she quickly drank two glasses of cool water to calm herself.

She read the messages left at the front desk from her brother and sister and her law partners, and sent a text message to each of them. Then she studied her notes. Satisfied that the trip wasn't a total loss, she contacted some of the others on her list and arranged to meet them. She had most of the information she needed to confirm her client's alibi with just a few phone calls.

Darlene was excited as she contemplated dinner with Mike. She decided to wear an off-the-shoulder chiffon dress that fit her body like a glove. She added pearl earrings, lipstick that was the same rose color of her dress, and a dab of perfume to complete her ensemble. Her hair hung in soft curls below her shoulders.

Darlene jumped when the phone rang a few minutes before seven. It was the front desk. She had a visitor. Darlene could barely contain her excitement. "I'll be right down," she said.

Mike stood facing the elevator when she stepped out

of it, and his eyes shone like brilliant stars. He handed her a bouquet of tea roses and kissed her cheek. "You are beautiful," he said.

"You look wonderful, Mike. I'm glad to be with you."

"Hey, that's my line." He walked with her to the desk and handed the bouquet to the clerk. "Please have someone put these in Ms. Cunningham's room."

"Yes, sir," the man said.

"We're going to Equestria. I like the atmosphere there, and you're so lovely you deserve a restaurant that is as beautiful as you."

"Thank you." She wanted to let him know how much his thoughtfulness had touched her, but no other words came.

He reached over and pressed her body to him. "Why are you nervous? I want to know where that sassy, rambunctious woman is hiding."

"I can't help you," she said, "because I don't know anyone like that."

He listed some of the smart-mouthed comments she'd made, adding, "Please don't do away with her. That woman whets my appetite." She wasn't about to reply to that.

He drove along Forest Hill Irene Road and stopped at a gray-and-red one-story building, surrounded by trees and shrubs. She knew before they reached the door that he was taking her to a special place.

"I'm sorry they don't have live music here," he said

as they followed the maître d' to their table. "We can go dancing afterward if you like."

"It's a beautiful place," she said. "I could sit here with you all evening."

"I hope you're trying to make me feel like a king, because that's what you're doing."

"Why not? Every woman wants a king."

"I think I'll stay on the safe side and not touch that one. What time does your flight leave tomorrow?"

"Three-twenty, which means I won't get to say good-bye to Boyd. I hate that."

"You want to stop by after dinner and spend half an hour with him? Then we can drop by the Cappricio, which is in the Peabody, catch some jazz and dance. What do you say?"

"I'd love that. Won't Boyd be about ready to go to bed when we finish here?"

"Hardly. He plays solitaire on his computer until midnight. Then he gets a book and starts reading. He's a very interesting man."

"I know," she said. "He's such a sweet man. There ought to be a lot of people like him."

"I gather he's under police protection."

"Please make sure nothing happens to him."

"I'll do what I can. He's all alone, but I plan to drop by to see him at least once a week as long as he's under police protection. When can I come to Maryland to see you? I mean, how much advance notice do you need?"

A frown marred her features. "Mike, my life isn't complicated."

"All right. Can I visit you next weekend? I'll get there Friday and leave on Sunday." She opened her mouth, but not a sound emerged. Her thoughts went to the only problem that might arise.

Mike's expression shifted as fast as mercury in a sudden heatwave. "Sorry for being presumptuous," he said. "But…"

She reached out and stroked his hand to reassure him. "I was trying to figure out what accommodations I could make so—"

He interrupted her. "You're kidding."

"No, I wasn't. If a man is coming to Frederick, Maryland, to see me, I have to put my best foot forward. My brother and sister, Clark and Tyra, will be after me to get organized and be mature, especially with a houseguest."

"You look plenty damned mature to me. I hope you ignore them."

"I do, and it drives them crazy."

"You haven't answered my question."

"Of course I'll be happy to see you next weekend. We have a big house. Usually, only Maggie our housekeeper and I are there. But if Clark knows a man is coming to visit me, you can bet he'll be there for the entire weekend. My sister Tyra is married and lives in Baltimore. If Clark gives you the third degree, I'm sure you'll let him know right away that you're as good at that as he is."

"Hmm. I haven't had much experience tangling with protective brothers."

"I *love* him, but I don't tell him that. A father wouldn't be as strict."

"Not to worry, Darlene. I haven't met a man who could make me cringe."

They finished a gourmet meal of steamed lobster with drawn butter, green peas, dauphin potatoes, braised pearl onions, green salad and caramel-rum soufflé. Afterward, as they were sipping espresso, he clasped her hand.

"I want to dance with you. If we don't leave soon, there won't be enough time to see Boyd and enjoy some live music."

"I'm ready," she said as she drained her coffee.

He held her hand as he stood and looked at her with an odd expression. "You said those same words to me as we were about to leave Boyd's earlier today. Are you sending me a subtle message, or is it merely a coincidence?"

"If I'm sending you a message, I'm not conscious of it. Let's go."

They left the restaurant holding hands. Before turning on the ignition, he telephoned Boyd. "Hello, this is Mike. How's it going? Great. Darlene and I are out on the town. She's leaving tomorrow and wants to say goodbye. Can you stand our company for ten minutes?"

"I can stand it for a lot longer than that," Boyd replied.

Once they arrived at his house, Boyd opened the door, stood back and looked at Darlene. A smile floated over his face. "One of the blessings of aging is being able to appreciate beautiful young women, platonic and safe though it may be. Come in, Darlene, and let me look at you." His gaze traveled over her, and then he looked at Mike. "You've got a prize there, Mike. Take care of her."

They drank some coffee and ate the Belgian chocolates that Boyd offered them while they talked.

"I don't offer these chocolates to anybody else," he assured them. "They're my favorites."

After several minutes, they stood to leave. Both of them embraced the older man. "If I write, will you answer?" Darlene asked him.

"Sure will. I answer the phone, too. Go with the angels," he told them.

Mike stood outside, holding her hand, until he heard the lock click. "That old man grows on me, but not the way you do. You're sinking into me like quicksand." He opened the front passenger door, walked around the car inspecting his tires, got in and was soon speeding toward the Peabody.

He gave his car keys to the hotel valet and led Darlene to the Lobby Bar. As they entered the bar the band played "Easy Living."

"Dance with me. I've wanted to hold you in my arms all day." After handing a waiter a note, he walked with her to the dance floor and opened his arms.

"I'm surprised that you didn't find an opportunity sooner," she said.

"There've been several, but I detest behaving like a lovestruck teenager." The song ended quickly. But before Mike could move his arms from her body, the beginning notes of the Beatles' "Something" reached her ears, and she melted into him.

"Watch it, sweetheart," he whispered. "I'm already at my boiling point as it is."

Darlene hadn't noticed Mike's amorousness. She had wanted to kiss him from the time she walked into Boyd's house that morning, but he had behaved then and since as if they were under his partner, Cody Johnson's, stern gaze.

"With your self-control, you can handle it. I love dancing with you, and I'm going to enjoy this."

"Go on and have fun. I'll see if it's everything I expected."

She snuggled closer. "You said I was beautiful. That's all I need."

He kissed the top of her head. "You started a fire, so you'd better think about how you'll put it out."

"I'm not worried," she said as his arm tightened around her. 'You'll protect me." She stood back to look into his face, and his heated attraction in it. She eased back into the cradle of his chest.

The haunting song ended, and Mike led her back to their table. "Let's have a glass of wine or something," she said. "I don't want this night to be over."

He ordered a vodka tonic for himself. "What would you like?"

"Vodka Collins, thank you," Darlene said.

The drinks came, and he raised his glass to her. "You're supposed to miss me the minute you get on that plane."

"I miss you just thinking about it."

She looked at him and glimpsed the blatant need blazing in his eyes. Stormy eyes. He immediately looked away, and she knew that he was embarrassed at having such naked desire. Without thinking about it, she grasped his hand. Her reward was a clear but silent question. She shifted her gaze away from him and sipped her drink.

Mike signaled for the waiter, paid the bill and reached for Darlene's hand. "Shall we go?"

Her entire body seemed to quicken, and goose pimples tingled across her bare skin. She stumbled a little as he helped her from her chair, and his arm slid around her shoulder.

"Easy, sweetheart. I won't let anything happen to you. Not now. Not ever. Trust me."

"I do," she whispered. "I don't know why, but I do."

He hadn't questioned his feelings as closely as he probably should have. But he knew he wouldn't get her out of his system, and with five or six hundred miles between them, he had to hold her as closely to him as he could while he had the chance.

Outside the door of her hotel room, he held out his hand for her key. She handed it to him without hesitation.

"May I come in?"

She immediately took his hand, opened the door, and led him inside the room. Through the window, his gaze captured the lights of the city reflecting off the Mississippi River.

"It's beautiful at night," he said. "And so are you."

"Should I get something from the minibar?" she asked.

He shook his head. "I'm fine." He had to get her to relax. "Do you have a terrace?"

She nodded and opened the door that led to the balcony. He stepped out on to the terrace, extended his hand to her and wrapped her in his arms. *Might as well put it on the table,* he told himself.

"You're nervous and shy," he said as he stroked her bare arm. "Not at all the feisty and sassy Darlene who was so irreverent yesterday. Can you tell me what's troubling you?"

She didn't speak for a few minutes, and he didn't press her. "I'm not all that worldly," she told him. "I've only had one boyfriend, and we parted about three months after... Well, it didn't work for me."

"I see."

"Do you?" she asked him.

He did. She wanted some assurance that he knew what she was referring to.

"You were disappointed in bed?"

"Uh-huh."

"Then you did the right thing. If the two of you couldn't make it work, then it wouldn't have been wise to continue the relationship. Are you still friends?"

She laid her head against his shoulder. "We're friendly when we see each other in public, but that's all."

"That's civilized. Very often, it's no one's fault."

She stepped back and looked at him. "You think so? I wasn't attracted to him as I am to you."

He tipped up her chin and stared into her eyes. Even in the darkness he could see the desire in her eyes, but there was fear, too. Still he wanted her. The thought that if he made love to her, he'd begin to need her made him uneasy.

He tilted his head down, flicked his tongue along the seam of her lips and pressed for entry. She opened her mouth and swallowed, sucking his tongue as she would a lollipop. The movements simulated an orgasm. Mike began to perspire, and he could feel his shirt sticking to his back. His blood coursed through his veins swiftly to his groin. He tried to step back from her, but she wouldn't let him.

"Do you want me to leave or what? Tell me what you want."

"I want you to kiss me."

"I *am* kissing you."

"You're not," she said, rubbing her hips against him. "Honey, my body aches. You know what I want."

He moved his hands toward the strapless bodice of

her dress, released her left breast, lifted it, fastened his mouth to the nipple and began to suckle her ravenously. "Mike, oh my," she said. She locked her legs around him and undulated her hips. He bulged against her body and did his best to let go of her, but she wouldn't allow him. He stepped back into the room, slammed the balcony door shut with his foot, and made it to the bed, where he placed her body underneath his.

"If you don't want to make love," he said, short of breath, "let me know now. I was on fire for you even before we danced. Darlene, honey. I won't push you into anything you don't want, but I am just a man."

He looked into her face and thought he would erupt right then, right there. She licked her lips and regarded him like a woman addicted. "I don't want you to leave me. Help me get out of this dress. Nobody makes love in a dress."

"What?" He told himself that if he laughed, he'd ruin the moment. Sitting up, he unzipped her dress, slid it over her hips and draped it across a chair. Then he kissed her bare belly, removed her shoes, stood and looked down at her.

"You're the most beautiful being I ever saw." He took off his clothes as fast as he could. He stood over her wearing only his briefs. He leaned down and kissed her. "May I?"

"Yes." She lifted her hips, and he removed her red bikini panties.

"Aren't you going to take that off?" She pointed to his briefs. "Let me do it." She moved to the edge of the bed and eased down his briefs. Wide-eyed and eager, she stroked him, watched him jump to full readiness, then leaned over and sucked him into her mouth.

"Hmm. You taste good. I never thought I'd like that." She realized that she might be misleading him. "I'm not experienced, Mike. I…I mean, I don't know much. But I…I need to be with you."

"Don't worry, darling. Just relax and follow my lead." He gazed at her beautiful body, the rounded hips and full bosom, and sucked in his breath. A smile spread across her face, sweet and so trusting.

He rested one knee on the bed, staring down at the treasure before him, his blood pulsing in his loins.

She opened her arms and licked her lips. "Come here." His body shook. He'd never wanted a woman so badly in his life. "Come, honey," she whispered and spread her legs.

He tumbled into her open arms and looked down at her. Could he possibly be in love with a woman he'd known less than three days?

Her hands caressed his back until he eased his body over hers, kissed her eyes, her cheeks, ears, nose and lips. He wanted to touch every inch of her, to make certain that she never wanted another man. She turned her face in a silent plea for his affection, and when she parted her lips, he thrust his tongue into her, but only for a second. Then his lips seared her neck, throat and her breasts. Her squirming told him what she wanted him to do to her, as he stroked her erect nipple.

"Honey, please. You know what I want."

She didn't have to beg. He wanted desperately to wrap his lips around her nipple, and when he pulled it into his mouth, she cried out.

"Yes. Oh, yes."

When his tongue touched her nipple, her hips swayed up to him, and she tried to throw her leg across him. She could hardly stand the heat building in her. "Mike, I'm so… I…I need you inside me. Please, I'm so hot."

But he charted his own course. Releasing her breast, he swirled his tongue in her navel, kissed the inside of her thighs and felt her tense. "Give yourself to me, sweetheart. I want to have it all. Relax and let me love you."

When he hooked her knees over his shoulders, she nearly panicked anticipating what he'd do next, but when he kissed his way from her knees to the top of her thighs and then sucked her clitoris, screams of pleasure poured out of her. He didn't linger, but made his way up her body.

"Take me in, baby. I can't wait any longer." She took him into her hands and brought him to her. He pushed for entrance.

"You said you'd had some experience, but there's a barrier here. Have you been penetrated?"

"I thought so."

"I'm not so sure. This may hurt. Do you want me to go on?"

She wrapped her arms around him as tightly as she could. "Yes. Yes. I need you."

He brushed her lips with his. "Relax as best you can."

He stroked her clitoris until he felt the liquid flow over his fingers. "Now. We'll go slowly." He pressed gently. She tried not to react to the pain. Finally, ignoring his warning to move slowly, she grasped his buttocks and swung her body up to him. She sighed and squirmed under the pressure. It had hurt. The worst pain she'd felt in her whole life.

"I'm so sorry," he said, kissing her eyes and her cheek.

"Are you all the way in?"

"Yes. I don't understand. You're a virgin?"

"A what? But—"

"Shh. We'll talk later," he murmured. He reignited the fire in her, sucking her nipples and massaging her clitoris until she again grabbed his buttocks and swung her body to his, getting the friction she needed.

As if convinced by her action that she was ready, he began long, slow thrusts, slowly increasing his strokes, whispering words of endearment, encouraging her. "That's it. Aw, sweetheart, yes. Love me, baby. Yes, just like that. Yeah!"

A strange heat began at the bottom of her feet, and then her thighs began to tremble. "Mike. Oh…I can't stand it." The squeezing and pulsating in her vagina wouldn't stop, and the feeling persisted such that if she didn't burst, she'd die.

"Yes, you can stand it, baby. I want you to give yourself to me. Don't struggle with it. Just concentrate on what I'm doing to you. Do you need it faster? Harder? Concentrate."

"I am. I am. Oh, I think I'm dying right now. Help me."

With a hand under her hips, he stroked powerfully, harder and faster. And then she felt herself clutch him, gripping him, and her whole body tingled. "That's it, baby. Oh, yes." He rocked her.

"I can't stand it. Mike, I'm dying." Her vagina tightened its hold on him, pumping and squeezing until he cried out. "You're mine. Mine, do you hear!" He gave her the essence of himself and collapsed.

"Are you all right?"

"Yes."

"Tell me the truth. I know you were having an orgasm, but did you come before I came? I couldn't hold out any longer."

"I…if there's any more, I'm not sure I can handle it. It was wonderful."

"Let me rest for a minute. Then we'll talk."

"Okay. Does it hurt every time?"

He stared down at her. "Did it hurt the other time?"

She shook her head. "No. It didn't."

A smile spread across his face. "Good. Darlene, I'm the only man who's ever been inside of you."

He rested his head on her shoulder, and she wrapped her arms around him. Suddenly, he rose up. "Excuse me a minute." He separated them, swung off the bed and headed toward the bathroom. He came back a few minutes later and handed her a warm, damp cloth.

"Use this to wash off." She stared at him with what must have been a quizzical expression. "Please, Darlene. It's important." She took the cloth, did as he said and looked around for a place to put it. But to her chagrin, he took it from her, looked first at it and then at her, and she'd never seen such a happy expression on his face.

"What is it?" she asked him.

"I wanted to be sure, and the stains on this cloth are proof. As I thought when I entered you, this was your first time." He disposed of the washcloth, got back into bed and put his arms around her.

"If you had known that you were still a virgin, would you have taken me here tonight?"

Darlene had to think about that one. "Yes," she said at last. "I would have, but I probably would have been more modest."

He kissed her shoulder and her breasts. "I hadn't given it a thought, and it wouldn't have mattered. But the thought that you have never been penetrated by another man but me just blew my mind. And, since you thought otherwise, I wanted evidence."

When his lips brushed over her breast, she felt a stirring deep inside. "Can we, uh…can we make love again tonight?" she asked him.

His eyes reflected his hope and excitement. "Yes, of course. But you're probably too sore."

"No, I'm not, and we won't see each other again until next weekend, so…"

His laughter floated through the room and, minutes later, he was driving them on the road to sweet paradise.

She knew he wanted to spend the night with her. But she imagined her sister Tyra wagging her finger, Maggie looking exasperated and Clark…Clark would be ready to take Mike on. With that thought, Darlene drifted off to sleep.

"I'd better be going," Mike said at about two o'clock the next morning.

"I'll call you before I leave," she said, wondering how she would feel away from him.

"I'll be here at eleven, to drive you to the airport."

And so he was. She couldn't understand his apparent disconnectedness on the drive to Memphis International Airport. He wasn't nervous, but he was not the man-in-control whom she had become accustomed to. As they approached the security area in the airport, and he could go no farther, he put her bag down, grasped her shoulders and looked into her eyes. "I hate it that you're leaving me. Promise me that you won't see any other man."

She reasoned that no sane woman would make such a promise to a man she'd known less that a week. "Mike, we've known each other less than a week."

From the expression on his face, she was fairly certain that he hadn't expected that response. "Considering what happened last night, time is irrelevant. I need to know that you're mine."

She reached up and kissed him quickly on the mouth. "There won't be anybody else, Mike. I'll call you when I get home."

He pulled her into his arms and demanded a fiery,

openmouthed kiss. "You're precious to me. Don't forget that."

"I won't." She left him standing there and made her way into the line for the security check.

Darlene unlocked the front door with her key, found Maggie in the kitchen and hugged her. "How was it?" Maggie asked, wiping her hands on her smock. Maggie rarely wore an apron.

"Fantastic," Darlene called back, already charging up the stairs to her room. She went to her desk and searched through the Rolodex until she found Edward Hathaway's number. Then sat down at her desk and dialed it.

"Hello, Edward, this is Darlene."

"Darlene! It's good to hear from you. What a nice surprise."

She didn't think as highly of him as she once had, and she was not in the mood for banalities. "Edward, I need to talk with you for a minute. Could we meet at Starbucks for a cup of coffee? I promise I won't keep you long."

"Sure. When?"

"Right now if you can make it." He'd think it one of her hasty, ill-conceived ideas, but he'd be wrong this time.

"Would you like me to come by for you?"

"Thanks, but I can walk there faster than you can drive here. See you shortly."

Edward Hathaway owed her an explanation, one that she would believe. She changed into a conservative but attractive summer dress, piled her hair on her head, added some big hoop gold earrings and dashed into the kitchen.

"I'm meeting somebody at Starbucks for a few minutes. I'll be back shortly, and we can talk then. I'm not eating there, just having coffee."

Edward waited for her at a back table. He stood when she entered the coffee shop.

"My goodness," he said as he leaned down to kiss her cheek. "You're glowing. You look fantastic."

"Thanks. I'm only having coffee."

He ordered coffee, and brought it to their table. "You're in a very sober mood, Darlene. What is it?"

She sipped the coffee, marveling that he remembered her preference for cinnamon. "I'm telling you more than you need to know, Edward, but I have no choice. What happened the night we went to bed? I had thought that you made love with me, but you didn't. What was that all about? What happened and why?"

He leaned back and looked her in the eye. "I've been expecting these questions. Almost immediately after we were in bed…no, even while I undressed you, I had the feeling that I had seduced a child. I know you were twenty-seven, but I realized that you were an innocent, that you didn't even know how to touch a man, and that your feigned sophistication was a cover-up."

"Why didn't you teach me?"

"I couldn't do that, because I had not decided what I wanted for us, whether I wanted our relationship to be exclusive. I didn't want to hurt you, and you had me to the point of explosion, so I got relief elsewhere. I knew that unless you were experienced, you wouldn't know the difference."

"But that didn't work for me and I needed much more."

"I'm glad of that, and I'm also glad that you found it."

"I didn't—"

"Yes, you have, and I'm not only glad but immensely pleased that you could share that with a man who cared more deeply than I."

She thought about that for a few minutes while she silently sipped coffee. "Thank you. I don't suppose many men would have done that. I was a flirt who loved to see the reaction that I could get from men. You were older than most men I'd dated, and you sent my ego sky-high. But after that disappointment, or maybe because of it, my attitude towards men changed. I still like to play, and I guess I'm still a flirt, though not intentionally. What I'm saying is that the experience with you changed me, and I'm grateful."

"You've changed, all right. I wish I were meeting you now for the first time, but that can't be. How's Tyra? Did she marry Whitley?"

"Yes. They live in Baltimore with his son, Andy, and his aunt. They're expecting a baby in about six weeks."

"How nice! Give them my best wishes."

Darlene stood. "I must be going. I got in from

Memphis a little less than two hours ago. All the best, Edward, and thanks."

She passed a newsstand, bought a copy of the *Maryland Journal* and headed home.

"I sure would like to know who you had to see the minute you got back in town," Maggie said to Darlene as soon as she entered the house.

Darlene hugged Maggie. "Oh, I had to check out a few things with an old flame."

"An old flame! You ain't had but one, and that one didn't last long before you sent him packing. Let's see how long this one hangs around." Maggie slipped an arm around Darlene's shoulder.

"How do you know there's someone?"

"Darlene, you're as transparent as glass. I'm looking at you. I hope for your sake that he's worth that look of delight on your face."

Chapter 4

It did not surprise Darlene to see Clark walk into the house later that day. He considered it his responsibility to watch over her. Because she loved her brother, she tolerated his controlling ways. She heard the key turn in the lock. "Want to bet that's Clark? Tyra is married and busy these days, thank goodness," she said to Maggie.

"Hi, there," Clark said to Darlene, bringing her into his arms for a hug. "I see you managed to get home. What were you doing in Memphis in the first place? Can't that law firm hire a private investigator?"

"The other partners didn't think the case was worth it, which is probably why they gave it to me in the first place. They didn't want me to go to Memphis, but nobody tells *me* where I can go. I may be the youngest in the firm, but I'm still a partner."

He took a bottle of beer from the refrigerator, grabbed a handful of potato chips, straddled a kitchen chair and sat down. "What else have you been up to, and don't say *nothing?* You haven't once protested the fact that I'm treating you as if you were a child. Could it be that, all of a sudden, you *realize* that you aren't?"

She walked over to him and patted his shoulder. "Don't bother to fish, Clark. It'll be a waste of your time."

He looked at Maggie, who was taking a roast from the oven to baste it. "Did she give you this same line, Maggie?"

Maggie rubbed her hands across the front of her apron. "She didn't dare give me a line. You know I can read Darlene like an open book. It's time you backed off, Clark. Darlene is a grown woman, and she's entitled to as much privacy as you are."

He drained the bottle of beer and got up. "I guess that puts me in my place. It also tells me something's going on. What time's dinner?"

"You're getting to be just like a Yankee. Dinner! Humph! What I'm cooking is supper, and that'll be ready at seven o'clock," Maggie said.

Clark patted Maggie's cheek. "I want you to know that eating at seven is a Yankee custom. Southerners eat dinner early."

"Yeah," Maggie said in the tone of one who has lost the point. "Whatever."

After dinner, Darlene and Clark helped Maggie clean the kitchen, and then Darlene raced upstairs, took a quick shower and crawled into bed. Anxiety had all but frayed her nerves, so much so that her skin tingled. Why didn't he call? Suddenly, she realized that she had promised to call *him* as soon as she got home. She laughed aloud and dialed his number.

"I haven't done a thing since you left me but wait for this call. I haven't even had dinner."

"I'm sorry," she said, "but I just remembered that I'm the one who was supposed to call."

"You were waiting for my call? Serves you right. Kiss me." She made the sound of a kiss.

"I'll see you Friday evening around seven. Don't meet me at the airport. It's bad enough that I'll have to kiss you in the presence of your family."

"Passengers at the airport won't care, but I can just see Clark getting in between us when he thinks you're about to kiss me."

"You're exaggerating. Besides, I haven't met a man who'd make that kind of mistake with me."

They talked for a while, neither willing to end the conversation.

"I spoke with Edward right after I got here," she said after a brief pause in the conversation.

"Who's Edward?"

She told him about her relationship with Edward.

"Was that necessary?"

"It was something that I was prepared to talk to him about," she said.

"He could have ended it. But he did the next best thing."

"I suppose so. But he should have told me that he didn't see me as someone to take seriously in a relationship. I'd never thought anything of flirting. But after that, my attitude has changed. I stopped playing with men. It is no longer fun."

"You had a moment of truth."

"After we talked, I felt better about the relationship."

"You were with him?"

"Yeah. I called him and told him I wanted to see him. I couldn't discuss that over the phone. I wanted him to look me in the eye."

"You're satisfied now that your disappointment had nothing to do with you?"

"I knew that before you took off my dress. Nothing about it was the same. Honey, if I had a lollipop, I'd give it to you."

"What? What the hell does that mean?"

"When I was little, my daddy used to reward me with a lollipop, because I loved them. I'd better get to sleep, because I have a ton of work tomorrow. Good night, honey.

"Good night, love."

Mike hung up and spent the next half hour musing over his conversation with Darlene. When first meeting her, he had thought that she possessed an innocent manner, but he couldn't have been further off the mark. What he'd observed, but had not correctly surmised, was that Darlene's insistence upon being truthful about everything had nothing to do with her naiveté. She joked and teased, but even in that, she didn't lie. What you saw was exactly what you got. She wanted to make love to him, and she let him know it. A woman without guile—she was a rarity, and he intended to treat her that way. There was much about her that he didn't know and should get to know before he got in deeper, and he meant to use the coming weekend to good advantage.

Darlene marched through the doors of Myrtle, Coppersmith & Cunningham, LLP, and headed for the third office on the right. "Hi, Ann," she called to her secretary. "I see the place is still here."

"It sure is, and your in-box is crammed. Say, what happened to you?"

Darlene paused. "What do you mean?"

"You're glowing. If I thought ninety-five-degree heat would make me look the way you do, I'd head South right now."

"There's nothing like the sun to make your cheeks rosy," Darlene said and rushed into her office to hide her embarrassment. Could everyone see what had transpired while in Memphis? She briefly glanced over at the voice-mail light blinking on her phone, checked her emails and went to the conference room for the regular Monday morning meeting.

"Apart from what must have been a trying weekend," Sam Myrtle began, "I hope you got something out of the trip."

"I got some important interviews, and I'm almost

certain we can forget about my client's alibi in Memphis. He's trying to throw me off. Everything I learned in Memphis about this case is counter to what my client says, and I don't want to represent him. You will see from my report that nothing I found sustains his assertion. He's lying, and he's covering up something."

Both Myrtle and Coppersmith lurched forward. "But Darlene," Sam said, "that's a very large retainer. You're willing to drop it?"

"Absolutely. If I cleared him, I wouldn't be able to sleep. I will not defend someone I know is guilty. Besides, since I don't believe him, I wouldn't be able to give him a first-class defense. I doubt the credibility of his alibi who came out of nowhere and volunteered to testify for my client."

"Hmm." Sam Myrtle wiped his glasses and pinched his nose. The man hated to pass up a hefty fee, especially since the firm's caseload was down. "We'll have to give this a lot of thought. That's a substantial sum of money."

"Yes," she said. "Yes, it is, but I don't think we want to be associated with this case."

After leaving work that day, Darlene was headed toward her car when she nearly tripped and fell on the sidewalk. A Good Samaritan grabbed her, steadied her and inquired about her well-being.

"I hope you aren't injured. How do you feel?" he asked her.

Something just didn't feel right. She'd passed that way every day and had never seen piles of debris there before. She looked at the man—tall, handsome and svelte. "Did you put that garbage on the sidewalk? Of course, I stumbled. I didn't expect to see it blocking my path."

"You could at least thank me for helping to break your fall."

Something wasn't right, so she changed tactics. "I'm sorry, sir, but I'm having a bad day."

"That's certainly understandable, Ms. Cunningham. Happens to all of us."

Her antenna shot up. "Did you call me Ms. Cunningham? Who's she?"

"W-well, you are," he stammered. "I mean, I…uh, was led…I mean, I thought you were."

She smiled. "Sorry to disappoint you, Mr…. What did you say your name was?"

"Pickney. Bradford Pickney." His facial expression let her know that he was trying to determine whether his name rang a bell with her.

It did, but she responded with a poker face. "I'm glad to meet you, Mr. Pickney. Have a great day."

The name Pickney was on the list of people she was to have interviewed in Memphis. She'd been unable to reach that person. *Hmm.* She intended to check it out as soon as she got home.

Darlene did not bother to mention to Clark that a man would be visiting her the coming weekend. She knew he'd grill her until she lost patience with him, and he would have a dozen questions ready for Mike. She knew she could also expect a family gathering, the purpose of which would be to scrutinize Mike. What a laugh! Mike was a master at dealing with interrogations. She wouldn't tell Clark, but she had to tell Maggie, who prepared their meals and kept the house.

"You mean to say he gon' be here for the weekend? Good thing you told me. Does he have any food preferences or allergies that you know of?" Darlene told her that she didn't think so. "Well, if you think enough of him to parade him past Clark and Tyra, I'd better pull out the stops. I'll plan a nice dinner for Friday evening."

She hugged Maggie. "I knew I could count on you." She started out of the dining room, where Maggie had been sewing, and stopped. "If my brother and my sister try to give him a hard time, they're going to get a surprise."

"Don't tell me he's tough."

"Yes, he is, and he can definitely hold his own."

"Glad to hear it," Maggie said. Still, Darlene noted a bit of uncertainty in Maggie's voice.

Mike didn't have any misgivings about his decision to spend a weekend with Darlene in Frederick, Maryland. He wanted to know her, and what better way to learn who she was than in her home? Their attraction had come hard and fast, shaking him up and causing him to question his thinking about getting involved with a woman he'd only briefly known. In the end, he'd had no choice. Every gesture she made drew him closer to her. And when he pulled out of her after the most electrifying and satisfying experience of his life, he'd have been a fool not to admit, at least to himself, that he belonged to her. He patted his shirt pocket for a package of cigarettes, remembered that he hadn't smoked in years, got up from his desk and went downstairs to his kitchen and opened a can of beer. A virgin. He was thirty-four years old, and that was the first time he had made love to a virgin. He still couldn't believe how she'd made him feel. As honest in bed with him as she was in ordinary conversation, her openness made pleasing her his passion and his mission. If only it wasn't a fluke. He could hardly wait to duplicate the experience again.

Friday finally arrived. He stepped into the waiting room at BWI Thurgood Marshall International Airport, and his gaze fell on her smile. He thought his heart had hit his sternum. He dropped his suitcase, lifted her into his arms and lowered his head. Her kiss, powerful and passionate, clouded his mind to his public surroundings. He lowered her to her feet and picked up his bag.

"I told you not to meet me."

"I know. But I wouldn't have missed this greeting for the world." She grasped his free hand. "I drove, because it's the easiest and fastest way to get home. We'll go directly to the suburbs."

"Have you missed me?" That kiss said she missed him a lot, but he wanted her to vocally acknowledge it.

"Uh-huh. You've even been invading my dreams."

He put the suitcase in the trunk of her car, opened the driver's door for her and held it.

"You mean you're going to sit beside me while I drive?" she asked sarcastically, as if the question itself was an insult to his male ego.

"Why not? I don't know one thing about this area." He got in beside her.

He liked the fact that she drove with confidence. Suddenly, he laughed. Why didn't that surprise him? It's what brought them together. Most people would have investigated before going to an unfamiliar address in a strange city, knocking on the door, and accepting the hospitality of a strange, elderly man.

"Are you afraid of anything?" he asked when she took the exit ramp at thirty miles an hour.

"Sure. I'm scared of worms and snakes."

Laughter poured out of him, partly because he was amused and partly because he was relieved that they'd made it safely off the highway. "Just checking."

She parked in front of the big white Georgian house in which she'd been born and turned to him. "We're here."

"You haven't given me any rules," he said, although he didn't need to be told how to behave. But he wanted a better idea of what to expect.

"Use your good judgment," she said, opened the door and hopped out.

She rang the doorbell and waited. "Maggie's like my mother, Mike. So I have to give her a chance to meet you at the door." She looked at him with a quizzical expression. "What's your exact title?"

"Lieutenant Michael Raines, but don't you—"

The door opened, and a slim, matronly looking woman gazed at him. "Come on in."

Darlene slipped an arm around Mike's waist in as possessive an act as he'd ever witnessed and looked up at him. "Maggie, this is Lieutenant Michael Raines, but please call him Mike. Mike, this is my surrogate mother, Mrs. Maggie Jenkins."

"I'm glad to meet you, Mrs. Jenkins," he managed to say facing the most thorough scrutiny he'd ever experienced.

"Likewise," she said. "Come here and let me look at you." She grinned and shook her head as if perplexed. He didn't know what to make of it.

Then she put her arms around him and hugged him. "You'll do. Looks like Darlene's finally grown up." He figured that meant he'd passed muster.

"I'll show you to your room," Darlene said. "Then I'll show you around the house. It's kind of big."

He followed her up the stairs to a room that had pale yellow walls, a beige carpet, walnut furniture and a chocolate comforter on a big sleigh bed. Its spaciousness appealed to him, and he felt at home.

"I like the room," he told her.

"It was our parents' bedroom, and we use it as a guest suite. It's very roomy, so I thought it would suit you. I hope Maggie didn't put you off."

"I didn't know what to think."

"Not to worry. With Maggie, what you see is just what you get. She's as honest as Lincoln."

"I finally got an inkling of that. Is this the only chance I'll get to kiss you?"

She gave him a withering look. "Trust me, Mike. I'm smarter than that." His eyebrows shot up as she brushed a quick kiss across his lips then hurried out of the room with the speed of a jungle cat. *In other words, get your libido under control, man, and keep it there.*

He looked around. So far, he'd seen a beautiful home with elegant but not overly ostentatious furnishings. When she first met Mike, she'd said her parents were physicians, and that she and her brother had been brought up by their older sister, Tyra. He had a feeling that it wasn't Clark who'd give him the third degree, but rather Darlene's sister Tyra. He settled into his room, and after changing into a pair of tan-colored pants and a yellow T-shirt, he strolled down the stairs.

"Mike, you want to come here in the kitchen for a minute?" He followed Maggie's voice straight to the kitchen. "Sit down here." She pointed to a straight-backed chair at the kitchen table. "Snack on this, since we're not having supper till Clark and Tyra get here. That'll be close to seven." She put a plate of buttermilk biscuits, country ham and fried green tomatoes in front of him, along with a mug of coffee. He said a silent thanks and relaxed.

"Did you say *snack?* For a guy who has to fend for himself in the kitchen, this is a full-course meal and a heavenly one at that. Thank you."

"What do you want in your coffee?"

"A little milk. Thank you. How long have you known Darlene?"

"Since she was seven. Are you serious about her?"

He savored one of the best biscuits he'd ever eaten. "Maggie, I would not have considered coming here if I wasn't serious. Darlene didn't invite me—I asked her if I could visit her this weekend, and she agreed. Yeah, I'm serious about her, and I think she's serious about me."

"That's what I thought. One good look at you, and I had you pegged as a man with integrity. You're a good guy, all right."

"I can see you took your time sizing me up. It takes a lot to make me squirm, and you came close to it."

"I wanted to be sure, 'cause when I make up my mind, I hardly ever change it."

"Want to see the rest of the place?" Darlene asked, announcing her presence. She knew Maggie would want to talk privately with Mike, and she hoped that whatever Maggie had on her mind had been laid to rest.

"I'd love it," Mike said, "soon as I finish this snack."

She walked with him through the house and then took him to the back garden, where they stood holding each other among the profusion of late summer flowers. "This garden must be beautiful on a midsummer moonlit night."

"It is, and I've done a lot of daydreaming out here. Oh!"

"What is it?"

"I hear Clark's car. Let's go inside."

"If he's curious, won't he come out here?"

"You're right. I have to stop being the baby sister."

"It's all right to be the baby sister, and still stand on your own. He'll appreciate that."

"I hope so." Getting Clark to abandon his big-brother role would take more than an adjustment on her part.

The back door opened. "So there you are," Clark said, striding directly to Mike. "Glad to meet you."

"Clark, this is Lieutenant Michael Raines. Mike, this is my brother, Clark Cunningham."

Mike extended his hand. "How are you, Clark? I'm glad to finally meet you in person?"

"And I'm glad to meet *you*. Tyra will be here in a few minutes." He looked at Darlene. "Mind if we all go inside? I'd like a drink. This has been a rough day."

Clark served drinks. They talked for about fifteen minutes when the doorbell rang. Tyra spent a minute with Maggie and then headed for the living room. Mike stood when she entered the room, and the minute her gaze landed on him, her face bloomed into a smile.

"I'm Tyra," she said and kissed Mike on the cheek.

"Supper's ready," Maggie called. "Do you want wine or iced tea?"

"Wine," said Darlene, Mike and Clark said in unison. Tyra was pregnant, and didn't drink.

Maggie ended the five-course meal with lemon soufflé. "We can have coffee in the living room," she said.

Tyra stood. "I'll get it. After that dinner you cooked, Maggie, you need to sit down."

"You won't catch me arguing with that," Maggie said.

Clark poured a brandy for himself after Mike declined, leaned back in his chair and draped his right ankle over his left knee. *Here it comes,* Darlene thought, and Clark did not disappoint her.

He looked at Mike. "It's never occurred to me that a way to get a woman's attention would be to detain her. Pretty clever, if you ask me."

Mike sat forward. "From the time my voice changed until now, I don't recall a single instance when I needed to detain her in order to get a woman. Not once. Besides, I insisted she remain in police protection in spite of my feelings for her. I wanted more than anything to let her go, but if I had she might have been in danger."

"What surprises me is that Darlene had the good sense to hold still long enough for you to catch her," Maggie said.

"Now you can apologize, Clark," Darlene said.

"No offense meant, Mike."

"None taken."

Tyra looked at Mike. "Why are men like this? I'm older than Clark. But when I was dating my husband, who Clark introduced me to, he made an absolute nuisance of himself, beating me to the door, waiting up until I got home and otherwise being a pest."

"I'm not so sure you want the answer right now," Clark said.

Laughter poured out of Mike. "No, you definitely don't—that is, if Clark's answer would be anything like mine."

The verbal sparring between Mike and Clark ceased when Clark saw that Mike wouldn't back down from a good fight and could give as good as he got. "I'd better head home," Tyra said. "It's getting late, and I have a forty-minute drive. If you have time, Mike, I'd love you to meet my husband Byron Whitley and my darling stepson. Byron will bring you back. I know you want to spend time with Darlene, so I'll understand if you can't make it this trip."

"He'll be back soon, Tyra. I have plans for him, and I didn't include Baltimore."

Tyra spread both hands, palms out. "Okay. No problem. I get the message."

When Mike looked at Darlene and smiled, Tyra thought, *My Lord, that man's smile is lethal. He's got charisma to burn.*

"I'll do my best to meet your family next time, Tyra," he said. "Thanks for inviting me."

Tyra went downstairs to the bathroom, and Darlene met her in the hall. "We have to spend time getting to know each other," she told her older sister. "Next time, we'll visit Byron and Andy."

Tyra enveloped Darlene in a hug. "I think he's terrific. You should enjoy him while he's here."

Tyra came back into the living room and said good-night, and Clark walked her to the door. No one had to tell Darlene that her brother and sister were comparing notes about Mike. Tyra liked him, and he had Clark's respect, albeit grudgingly so.

"Good night, you two," Clark said. "Don't stay up all night."

"Good night," Maggie called to them as she headed up the stairs.

"My goodness," Darlene said to Mike. "Something must be out of kilter. They're all behaving so nicely. You didn't brainwash them, did you?"

"You have a wonderful family, and they obviously love you very much. I thought Clark might give me a hard time, but he only wants to test my mettle."

"After the response you gave him, he'd have been foolish to try getting the better of you, and Clark is not foolish."

"I think it's best that I don't sit down here with you. It's too tempting not to take you in my arms and—"

"You mean you're planning to go to bed and not kiss me? Well, I do not plan to cooperate with that."

He picked her up, put her in his lap and let his hands roam over her body. "Hey, I didn't mean for you to light a fire."

"Do you think you can kiss me and I'll get one second of sleep tonight knowing you're sleeping under the same roof as I am?"

"Just a little," she said, as he captured her mouth. She parted her lips, and he plunged into her. The minute she tasted him, her blood began a mad rush south. She grabbed his hand and rubbed her nipple with it. As if in a panic, he jumped up, put her on her feet and pushed her gently from him.

"If Maggie or Clark had come down those steps right then, what would you have done? We'll get our moment, sweetheart, but definitely not like this."

He sat down with her, and she rested her head on his shoulder. "I confess I wasn't thinking."

His laughter wrapped around her like a warm blanket. "That's definitely an understatement, sweetheart." He encircled her in a warm embrace, and she kissed his neck, relaxed and happy.

"Would you believe what happened to me the afternoon I got home?" she asked him.

He said he wouldn't.

"After I spoke with Edward, I had a strange encounter." She related to him the incident with Bradford Pickney. Mike sat up straight, and she knew he was about to drop a bomb.

"I arrested a woman with the same last name. Why would that man be interested in you the day you returned from Memphis?"

"I'm trying to figure that out."

"In my business, there are no coincidences, Darlene."

"Evidently not. One of the people I was supposed to have interviewed was named Pickney, but she didn't answer her phone, although I called that number several times."

"Do you remember her first name?"

"Madeline, I think."

"She didn't answer because she is in jail for jury tampering. Hmm. What's your client's name?"

"Frank, Albert Frank."

"If Madeline's married, check her maiden name."

She looked at Mike quizzically. "I'm a detective, remember?" he said.

"Thanks, Mike. Do you mind if we stop by my office tomorrow morning? I should be able to check on that in about half an hour."

"Don't mind a bit. Let's call it a night."

She clasped him to her body, parted her lips over his and pulled him into her. Then, just as quickly, she released him.

"Good night, love. See you at about seven-thirty," she said and ran up the stairs. She wanted so badly to spend the night in his arms, but she knew that would be the wrong move.

Darlene walked into the kitchen at seven the next morning and found Maggie there with breakfast well underway. "Darlene, are you sure about this man? Don't think you can play with him, because he won't stand for it."

"I haven't known him long, Maggie, but I know he's the one. I knew it the first time I looked at him. At first, it scared me to death. I've never reacted to a man that way. So, I am definitely not playing with him. I want him to be the father of my children."

"Well, that's a mouthful. Whatever happened to Edward what's-his-name?"

"He was mature, sophisticated, an accomplished lawyer, everything that I wanted, Maggie. But when it came down to it, it didn't work for me. He's a decent, respectable man, but I don't feel about him the way I feel about Mike. Nowhere near it."

"You take good care of this, Darlene. He's first-class, and he cares about you."

"I know, Maggie. I grew up the minute he put his hands on me. So don't worry. I respect him, and I'm in it as deeply as he is."

"All right, but you protect that relationship. Give, but not foolishly. You hear?"

"Something smells good." At the sound of Mike's voice, Darlene whirled around and bumped into Clark.

"Sure does," Clark said. "While you two stare at each other, I'll set the table."

"I thought you were frying catfish this morning," Darlene said to Clark.

"I was going to, but when I remembered that I hadn't had any of Maggie's biscuits lately, I turned over and went back to sleep."

"We gon' eat right here in the kitchen," Maggie said. "Mike's a guest, but he isn't company. I'm scrambling eggs, and you know how long that takes."

Mike looked at the fried country ham, sausage, biscuits, scrambled eggs, pancakes and mixed fresh fruit that Maggie put on the table. "Keep this up, Maggie, and I'll be here every weekend." He looked at Clark. "How do you stay so fit eating like this?"

Clark bunched his shoulders in a shrug. "When I still lived here full-time, I practically killed myself exercising. Now I'm only here on weekends, and I try to stop eating when I get full."

"I don't see how you do that. I could sit here and eat till noon."

Darlene was pleased that Clark had accepted Mike and wouldn't interfere with their relationship. "But you won't," she said. "I don't date pudgy guys."

Mike was reaching for his fifth biscuit, but he withdrew his hand. "What's a guy to do? I don't believe in overindulging."

The round of laughter blessed her ears. Immediately, she sobered. *Please, God. Don't let anything happen to take him away from me.*

Ten o'clock found Darlene and Mike entering the offices of Myrtle, Coppersmith & Cunningham. "Someone's here," Darlene said when she saw a light from under the door. "Come on. I'd like to introduce you." They walked down the corridor until she reached Sam Myrtle's office and knocked.

"Come in."

She walked in and waited for Mike to follow her. "Hi, Sam. This is Lieutenant Raines, a detective in the Memphis Police Department. Mike, this is Samuel Myrtle, my senior partner." The two men shook hands and greeted each other. "Sam, do you have any more files on the Frank case? Looking through my notes, I can't seem to find one of the witnesses maiden name. She's married."

"Hmm. Do you think that's relevant?"

She glanced at Mike, who leaned against the doorjamb in a half slouch. "He says it's relevant." She pointed toward Mike.

Myrtle appeared skeptical, but he turned on his computer, searched through a file. "Lorraine Pickney Frank." When both Darlene and Mike gasped, Myrtle sat straighter, his attention riveted. "You know somebody else with that middle name?"

"Yeah," Mike said. "Madeline Pickney, could possibly be a twin, considering their names."

"She was on the list of people Mrs. Frank suggested I interview in Memphis, and a man named Bradford Pickney intercepted me the day I got back here," Darlene said.

Sam Myrtle removed his glasses and pinched his nose several times. "This doesn't look good, especially since you don't think you're alibi witness is reliable."

"A witness who suddenly volunteers is always suspicious," Mike said. "If I were on the case, I'd look into that witness. If you don't mind my saying it, begin with the premise that nobody involved in a case is completely truthful. Attorneys begin with the premise that you are innocent until proven guilty, depending on which side you're on."

Sam shook his head. "I didn't think we needed a detective, but I'm not so sure now. Will you be here for a while, Detective?"

"I'm here for the weekend," he said.

* * *

Later, when they got into Darlene's car, Mike began to discuss the case with Darlene. "I'd be glad to stay a day longer and help with the case if you want me to. This thing smells from here to Memphis."

"Thanks, Mike, but it would be unethical of me to allow you to do my work. You've given both me and Sam invaluable information, for which I'm grateful. But I know I can handle this. I have to believe in myself, Mike, and that means standing on my own two feet."

"All right. Let's drop this for the time being. I want to see what Frederick is like."

"At your service," she said, hoping to lighten the mood. Frederick is a complicated city. During the Civil War, it didn't go with either the North or the South, and today it's not really Southern nor Northern—like most of Maryland. The city celebrates a number of African-American heroes, beginning with Benjamin Banneker, the first great black scientist and mathematician this country produced. You'll find memorials to him in many cities. Also, the official Francis Scott Key portrait was painted by an African-American son of Frederick."

She drove along Bentz Street and slowed down when she reached number 121 South Bentz Street. I wanted you to see this house," she said. "It was built by Roger Brooke Taney, the Supreme Court Chief Justice who wrote the Dred Scott decision. I always spit at that house when I pass it. That decision held that slaves of African descent and their descendants were not protected by the

United States Constitution, had no recourse to law and could not be citizens.

"On the other hand, we have monuments to Barbara Fritchie, Rose Hill Manor, the National Shrine of Elizabeth Ann Seton, and the Battle of Gettysburg. So it's not all bad," she said. "Frederick and its environs have a wonderful history."

"Do you like it here so much that you wouldn't want to live any other place?" he asked. The soberness of his voice stunned her.

"I could live anywhere…if…if I was happy, Mike." This time, it was her own seriousness, her own truth, that unsettled her.

Chapter 5

Walking along Market Street in historic Frederick, Mike marveled at the town's uniqueness and how different it was from Memphis. So many of the houses were colonial. He had the feeling of being in two vastly different eras. Realizing that he'd been holding Darlene's hand tightly, he loosened his grip.

"What's the matter?" she asked, her face bearing an expression of concern.

He was about to say "Nothing," but he knew that wasn't true. "Let's talk when we get back home. Right now, I want to experience this city. It's so different from the South. It seems more like New England."

"Old Frederick is, because it's about the same as it was in the late eighteenth century. I'm glad you're enjoying it. I never have time to appreciate its history, so this is a treat for me, too."

At Patrick Street, they strolled over to Canal Street, where she'd parked her car. "Let's go home, Darlene." She gazed up at him with an inquiring expression, then evidently decided not to question him and took out her car keys.

"Okay."

He held her hand as they walked into the house. He led her to the living room. "Let's sit here. I need to talk with you." He didn't believe in postponing important issues, and this was important to him.

"Would you like something to drink?" she asked.

He shook his head. "Nothing. I want us to talk, Darlene. You and I are in similar fields. I know my job, and I accept that you know yours. But you've made it clear that when it comes to your work, you'd rather not hear my advice or have me interfere in your work, and not even when you're about to make a colossal mistake."

"Now, wait a minute, Mike. You don't know. And what if I do want to stand on my own? If I didn't know you, what would I do?"

"I hope you'd talk to a detective or a private investigator. You don't know everything. But that's not what this is about. If we're going to stay together, you have to stop being on the defensive. You have to trust me."

"Look, I was twenty-nine-years old when you met me, and nobody made me according to your directions. I mean—"

"Darlene, for heaven's sake, be careful what you say.

I'm trying to make you see that you and I have to find common ground. Otherwise we—"

"I hope you don't mind me interfering here," Maggie said, "and if you do, I'm gon' talk anyhow." She took a seat opposite them. "I've been listening to this argument, and I know where it comes from. Darlene, you have to stop looking at Mike as being controlling. He's a man, and men have a strong need to protect the women they care for." Darlene opened her mouth as if to speak, but Maggie raised her hand. "You can talk after I finish.

"Mike cares a lot for you, and you feel the same way about him. So don't be foolish and destroy what looks to me like a beautiful thing. Anybody can see how you feel about each other. Why do you think Clark and Tyra are giving you so much space? Darlene, you've spent so much time proving to Clark, Tyra and me that you're grown up and you can run your own life and trying to prove to those men you work with that you're a good lawyer that you're taking the same attitude with Mike. Stop looking at him as a threat. He's a man, and seeing *that* shouldn't make you defensive."

She looked at Mike. "Ease up, Mike. You're the second man Darlene ever brought to this house, and the first to spend the night. The other one came once and that was for Thanksgiving dinner. Darlene has to learn that she can no longer lower her lashes, flirt and use her charm to get what she wants. Teach her to deal with you as an equal. And Darlene, you will soon learn that a man hurts the same as a woman, only it goes deeper and lasts much longer.

"I left your supper on the stove. Dessert's in the refrigerator, and the table's set in the kitchen. I'm going to the movies, and I'll be back around eleven-thirty. That should give you plenty of time to fix things between you. And I mean fix it."

She got up and headed for the front door, and although he was still trying to absorb the tongue-lashing she'd given them, he had the presence of mind to walk to the door. "It's dark already. Are you taking a taxi?"

"The bus stops half a block from the theater," Maggie said.

"Wait a minute." Maybe Frederick was different from Memphis, but prevention beat cure any day. "Do you have the phone number for a taxi?" he called to Darlene. She gave him one. He dialed it, called the taxi. "At least you didn't tell me to mind my business."

"Be patient, Mike. You'll find it well worth your while."

"I know that, Maggie. The youngest child in the family is always spoiled and precocious."

"She was. Her mother said she walked at eight months, toilet-trained herself and knew the alphabet and how to count before she was three. She's always been precocious. But since you've been here, I've seen some marked changes in her. Clark and Tyra said the same. She's more thoughtful."

"Here's your taxi." He opened the door and walked out to the taxi with her. After paying the cabbie, he handed Maggie a ten-dollar bill. "Take a taxi back." She reached up, kissed his cheek and ducked her head back in the cab. He was certain that he saw appreciation in her eyes.

Inside the house, he found Darlene sitting as he'd left her. "You're very pensive," he said, sitting down and easing an arm around her.

She scooted closer to him and rested her head on his shoulder. "Do you think I'm contentious?"

"No, I don't. I think you need to learn to compromise. We'll have disagreements, but if both of us insist on having our way, we won't be happy together. I'm hungry."

He took his plate from the table setting and went to the stove. "Let's see. Chicken and dumplings, string beans, a carrot soufflé and corn bread. Oh, boy!" He waited until Darlene served herself and joined him. "Do you usually say grace?" he asked her.

"When I remember to do it, I do."

He said the grace. "I want my kids to say the grace before they eat and their prayers before they go to bed. That's the least I can teach them."

"Can you come back next weekend?" she asked, startling him so completely that his fork clattered against his plate.

"You want me to?"

"If it's inconvenient, but—"

"Of course I want to come back next weekend, and I will."

She looked at him with a diffidence that he didn't associate with her. "Because of me or for Maggie's cooking?"

Another surprise. "I certainly hope you meant that to be funny. If you need an answer, I'll be here for you, not for food."

"Sorry, but Maggie gave me such a jolt that I...I don't know. I was thinking about me and...and what I wanted and didn't want. Maybe you can write down a few questions that I can ask that witness."

His head jerked up. "Sure. I'll be glad to. According to the answers you get, you may want to follow up."

"What kind of questions are important?" she asked him.

He restrained the deep sigh of relief that nearly escaped him. He wanted to avoid anything that would compromise the case. "Places she's traveled in the last six months, her occupation, her siblings and other close family members, questions that flow from her answers. That's just off the top of my head."

"I...uh...I can't wait to see what you'll come up with after you've given it a lot of thought."

He hoped he was wrong, but he had a suspicion that she didn't take his work seriously. "Darlene, I've been a detective since I was twenty-six. I'll be thirty-five in January so that's nine years in the job."

She patted his knee. "You're getting old. Why did you decide to be a detective?"

He leaned back, comfortable with himself and with the topic. They didn't really know each other, and he suspected that was their problem. This exchange was overdue. "With two degrees in criminology, there wasn't much else I could do, since I didn't plan to teach or work in a prison. I've wanted to be a detective since I was eight and my favorite stories and books were by Arthur Conan Doyle and Erle Stanley Gardner."

"I'm glad you're a detective. If you weren't, I wouldn't have met you."

He stroked her arm. "Sure you would have. You were mine from the day you were born."

She bolted upright. "I didn't say I was yours."

He pulled her back into his arms. "You didn't have to say it. Action speaks louder than words ever will."

He knew that she was only half kidding, that she didn't think she wanted to *belong* to a man. Still fighting for independence, was she? He'd put an end to that. "If you don't belong to me, I'd be foolish to allow myself to belong to you, wouldn't I?" he said.

She moved away from him and stared into his face, her own face marred by a deep frown. "Are you telling me that you belong to me? Is that what you're saying?"

"I want to," he said, "but I'm not stupid. There isn't a snowball's chance in hell that I'd let myself care for a woman who didn't care for me. I might for a few days, but then I'd give myself a good kick in the behind, and she'd be history."

She lowered her lashes and then raised them slowly in a blatant act of flirtation. "Don't count on my not caring. I don't see that in my future. At least, not now."

"At least not now, huh? Come here, woman!"

* * *

Darlene rimmed her lips with the tip of her tongue, looked at his mouth and then slowly raised her gaze to meet his eyes, eyes that seemed to vibrate with passion. "You talking to me?" she said, all the while moving her mouth closer to his.

"Yeah!"

She didn't know how or when it happened, but his hands were all over her, his long fingers heating her to boiling point while his magic tongue danced in and out of her mouth, showing her what she'd get in the minutes to come. He pulled his tongue out of her mouth and brushed his lips over her eyes, face, ears and neck, but she had to have more.

"Kiss me, Mike. I need you to—"

"Tell me what you want." He stared into her eyes as his fingers teased the flesh of her bare arms, and every place he touched seemed to explode into a blaze. "Tell me."

"I…I want you in me, deep, as far as you can go." His mouth covered hers, and he plunged his tongue into her. Exasperated, she grabbed his hand and stroked the nipple of her left breast, hard and almost ruthlessly. "Kiss me. Why don't you kiss me?" she moaned.

"Open this thing and let me at it," he said, his voice urgent as his hot breath fanned her skin.

She shoved his hand into her blouse and released her breast. He sucked the nipple into his mouth. Her cry could be heard all over the house, and with that encouragement, he picked her up and carried her to his room.

"How do you get out of this thing?" he asked after kicking the door closed. She unbuttoned the top three buttons, pulled the blouse over her head, tossed it across the room, unzipped her skirt and let it fall to the floor. When, in his haste, he pulled her bra off, his fingers skimmed over her breast, grazing her nipples and sending hot darts of electricity throughout her body. He stared into her eyes, and when she wet her lips, he bent to her breast, sucked an erect nipple into his mouth and slipped his left hand into her bikini panties.

"Ooh," she moaned when he began rubbing her erect clitoris. "Why don't you just get in me?"

"Because I want you to enjoy this."

"I am. I will. I'll die if you don't get in me now."

Next thing she knew, he had her across the bed, pulled her hips to the edge of it, hooked her knees across his shoulders and was flicking at the edge of her vulva with his sweet tongue. "Stop teasing me. I can't stand this."

"Don't you like it?"

"I love it." He sucked on her clitoris. Frantic, she swung her hips up to him just as he shoved his tongue into her. Heat swirled at the bottom of her feet and, this time, she knew what to expect. "Please Mike. I'll come before you get in me."

He stripped himself, pulled a condom from under the pillow and prepared to join her. But before he put on the condom, she remembered the pleasure he seemed to get from the intimate kiss she gave him the last time they made love. So she sat up, took him into her hands, stroked him and then leaned forward and sucked him into her mouth, enjoying him as if sucking on a lollipop. Suddenly, he grabbed her shoulders and pushed her away.

"I thought you liked that."

"I love it, but you almost made me climax, and I don't want that to happen yet." He joined her and began an onslaught on her body, kissing, stroking and teasing until she was nearly out of her mind.

"Get in me, honey. You're driving me crazy."

"All right." He handed her the condom, and she sheathed him, marveling at his size, his hardness and the way he made her feel. He slipped into her, and with one arm around her shoulder and the other around her hips, he smiled down at her. She thought she'd go out of her mind. Then he unleashed his power, and he was over her, under her, in her and all around her, filling her, emptying her, molding her body, heart and mind, making her his.

"Who do you belong to?" He asked the question as her insides began to erupt in what seemed like an earthquake. "Tell me. Whose woman are you?"

"Yours," she moaned. "You know I'm yours. Give it to me harder. Stop playing with me."

"I'm not playing with you. Be patient, love. It's coming. Oh, yes!"

He seemed to fling her up and then toss her back down, until she felt herself grip him with such force that he paused as if glued to her. And then the all-powerful release.

At that moment, he shouted, "You're mine, and I'm not letting you go." His tremors shook her, and he collapsed, letting his elbows take his weight.

Neither of them spoke, and she knew that, like her, Mike was absorbing the impact of what they'd just done and what it meant. To her, at least, it meant forever, and she prayed that she hadn't made a mistake, because an error of such gargantuan proportions would surely ruin her life. She hadn't experienced true love in the past, and she couldn't swear that that was what she was feeling right then, but she knew that whatever it was, it had a powerful hold on her.

"How do you feel?"

She told him the truth. "I don't know. This goes far beyond what I felt with you in Memphis. It was…I guess it was natural, and it…it was as if I didn't exist anymore. I was you. Oh, I don't know what I'm saying. It was incredible, but at times I thought I was about to die."

He kissed her nose and held her closer. "The better we know and understand each other's needs, the better it should get."

Her eyes widened. "You mean you're planning to make a sex fiend out of me?"

His eyes sparkled, and a grin crawled over his face. "I'm damned well going to do my best."

She whacked his butt, raised her right knee and winked. "Two can play that game."

"Right, but I've been playing it longer than you have."

Her eyebrows shot up. He was hard and moving. She wrapped her arms around him and prepared herself for another trip to paradise.

Shortly after noon the next day, Sunday, she stood at the front door preparing to drive Mike to BWI Thurgood Marshall International Airport. Maggie joined them and handed Mike a package.

"Put this in your bag," she said to Mike. "It'll keep nice and fresh till you get home. When you coming back?"

"Next weekend."

Maggie nodded her head as she gazed at him. "Good. Very good. You didn't say so, but I can see that you straightened things out. Never throw God's blessings back at him. It's not a smart thing to do. Bless you." She kissed his cheek and left them.

"If she likes you, she shouldn't make it so obvious," Darlene grumbled. "Anybody'd think she wants to get rid of me."

"Look at it this way," Mike said as they headed for the airport in her car. "She knows that sooner or later some guy is going to get you, and she'd rather I was that guy. Don't park," he said when they arrived at the airport. "Kiss me right here. I'll see you next Friday afternoon, and in the meantime see that no man stops within thirty feet of you."

"What?"

"Well, ten feet." He pressed a hard kiss to her lips,

reached for his bag, jumped out of the car and didn't look back.

In a moment of inspiration, she realized that he was vulnerable and hadn't had much experience with vulnerability. *Well, neither have I, honey, and I'm learning to deal with it.*

Back in Memphis, Mike returned to his daily routine, although some of the spice had gone out of it, and he knew why. Minutes seemed like hours and hours like days as the week crawled by. He satisfied himself that Darlene's client was connected to the Pickney woman in the sense that they had stumbled onto a family of polished thieves. Darlene's client and her witness were unaware that one of their relatives was in a Memphis jail, or Darlene would not have been told to get in touch with her as a corroborative witness. Who knew what else this family of grifters was involved in?

Boyd Farmer was the lone witness who could bring the thieves to justice and Mike was determined that he make to trial. That evening. Mike drove out to Boyd's house carrying two roast-beef dinners and a quart of butter-pecan ice cream.

"Come in. Haven't seen you in ages," Boyd said.

"I know," Mike answered, although he didn't consider eleven days such a long time. "I brought us some supper. Thought we'd play a little gin. You up to it?"

"What'd you bring to eat? The woman who looks after the place quit. She didn't believe my story that nobody was allowed to enter or leave here. I don't much believe it, either."

"Why not? That's how we met." Mike said. He went into the kitchen and put the food on the counter and the ice cream in the freezer compartment of the refrigerator.

"Darlene called me twice," Boyd said. "She's the sweetest woman I've met in years. I wish I had a daughter like her."

Mike regarded Boyd carefully. "We'd better eat before this stuff gets cold. Who's doing your shopping?"

"I am. Who else? I'm not a baby. At seventy-one, I'm a better man than some of these young Turks around here. I put a few beers in the bottom of the refrigerator in case you came by one evening."

Mike cocked an ear. Young Turks, eh? One of these days he'd find out who Boyd Farmer really was. Foolish, he definitely was not, no matter what anybody said.

Boyd set the table, opened a bottle of beer and placed it where Mike was to sit. "I used to be a pretty good cook when I was young and entertained girlfriends, but I'm not doing fancy cooking for me to eat by myself. I just want to get full."

"Solid reasoning," Mike said and sat down.

After they finished the meal, Mike cleaned the kitchen and went into the living room, where Boyd was shuffling the cards. He put the cards down, looked at Mike. "I wouldn't mind having you for a son, either."

Mike swallowed rapidly and resisted the urge to pat the old man's hand. "I'm pleased, Boyd."

"Now, when I think of you, Darlene's there with you. Aren't you going to see her?"

Mike thought for a few minutes. Hadn't he come to regard the man as a friend? Why shouldn't he share his feelings with him? "I spent the weekend with her, Boyd. So stop worrying about us. We're working on it."

Boyd's face beamed in a glowing smile. "Wonderful. I knew you could recognize a fine woman when you saw one. Deal."

Mike drove home hours later thinking that no matter what game they played, be it gin, pinochle, or blackjack, Boyd managed to win. He had discovered that he enjoyed the man's company, that he could relax and be himself. And in his line of work, that was a luxury. Boyd neither asked anything of him nor expected anything; he merely accepted such friendship as Mike had to give.

"The guy is growing on me," Mike said to himself. Sometimes he wondered what his life would have been like if he hadn't lost his parents four days after he went to college. A deep sigh flowed out of him. No point in reliving the past. His life was his job, and lately that hadn't been so bad, he thought. He'd received three rewards from that job—getting to knowing Darlene and Boyd, and a promotion to chief of his unit. Not bad for six weeks of torture.

Friday finally arrived, and he wanted to fly on his own wings to Frederick, Maryland. "Calm down, man," he told himself. "Put your feet on the ground and keep them there." But when he saw her running to meet him with her arms widespread and a smile blooming on her face, he said to hell with propriety, dashed to meet her, brought her to him and nourished himself on the loving she offered.

"This was the longest week I ever lived," he said as they walked arm in arm to her car.

"It couldn't have been longer than mine, Mike. I'm practically a basket case. Every night, I sleep for an hour, wake up and start waiting for daybreak."

"Now it'll be my turn, 'cause I don't expect to sleep with you down the hall from me."

She giggled, or he thought she did. "If Maggie's so fond of you, maybe you can bribe her to go to the all-night movie, and I can—"

"I hope you're joking. She'd send me straight back to Memphis quicker than you can say Michael Raines. No, sir. I'm staying on Maggie's good side. How do you think she'll react if we don't eat at home tonight?"

"Oh. I'm sure she's planned something for you."

"I promised to visit Tyra when I came back, and something tells me I was a bit rash in making that promise. What do you say we drive there now? See if she's home. We don't have to stay too long, we can eat dinner with Maggie and—"

"Why not eat dinner with Maggie and then drive over to visit Tyra?" She gave him Tyra's phone number, and he dialed it on his cell phone. "Hello. May I please speak with Mrs. Whitley?"

"Just a minute," a deep male voice said. "I'll get her."

"Hello, Tyra. This is Mike Raines. I promised to visit

you and your family on my next trip here to see Darlene. I'm here to keep my word. Darlene suggests we see you this evening after dinner at home with Maggie. If that doesn't sit well with you—"

"That will be fine, Mike. I hope you can get here before Andy, our son, goes to bed."

He told her that he'd try, hung up and then turned to Darlene. "This is great. By midnight, when we come back home, we'll be too tired to think about getting busy."

She took a sharp turn, glanced toward him and let the Volkswagen speed past seventy. "I hope you know you're speaking for yourself."

He settled back in the soft, leather seat, comfortable and happy. "All right. *You* bribe Maggie. I'm doing no such thing."

"Y'all not gon' have good weather tomorrow," Maggie said when they walked into the house. He dropped his bag, hugged Maggie and told her of their plans to visit Tyra.

"I'm so glad. I think you'll like Byron. Go on up to your room and put your bags up there."

Halfway up the stairs, he called down to Darlene. "What are you wearing this evening?"

"A long-sleeved red dress. You can come as you are."

He got a shower, dried off and lay across the bed. A knock from somewhere in the distance awakened him two hours later. He scrambled into his clothes, rushed down the stairs and joined Darlene and Maggie for dinner in the dining room.

"I haven't been sleeping too well," he explained. "The minute I touched that bed, I was out. Please don't think I was being deliberately rude."

"We don't," Darlene said. "I, for one, guessed right."

"It wasn't my business," Maggie said. "I figured you were tired and you'd come down when you felt like it, though I *was* getting kinda antsy about my dinner spoiling." She patted his shoulder. "I hope you got a good rest."

"I did. Thank you." He stopped eating and looked closely at Maggie, a woman who had openly scrutinized him on sight, then accepted him for whatever it was that she saw in him. "You're not old enough to be my mother," he told her, "but you'd make me the kind of big sister that I always wanted. I get a good feeling around you."

"Those words mean a lot to me, Mike, more than I can tell you." She looked away from them, and he knew she was trying to maintain her composure. "What time y'all supposed to be at Tyra's?"

"About an hour and a quarter from now," Darlene said. "I hope you don't mind cleaning the kitchen tonight."

"I don't. Y'all have a good time, and give Andy a hug for me. I declare he is the most loveable little devil."

* * *

It amazed Darlene that her brother-in-law, Byron, and Mike got on so well—too well, in fact.

"It must be a relief to be able to discuss your case with someone you trust. My firm pays good money for the services of a good private detective," Byron said to Darlene.

She wished Byron had kept his thoughts to himself. The quiet that accompanied her non-response spoke volumes, but she was not about to change her attitude for the sake of pleasant conversation. And as she drove home, Mike commented on it.

"Byron was embarrassed when you didn't agree with his comment about working with a detective who you trust. You surprised me, too."

"I thought you and I had settled that," she replied.

"So did I. But it seems that we haven't."

She did not want to beat a horse to death again. She slowed down and switched to the right lane. "Mike, let's be clear that we deal with this working-together relationship on a case-by-case basis? Sometimes I will ask you for help, and at other times, I will rely on my own judgment. Incidentally, the questions you suggested I ask produced some telling results. It only confirms my belief that I should drop this case. I haven't turned in my report to Sam yet, because I wanted you to read it."

"Is it in your office?"

"No. I brought it home. My client's alibi is his aunt.

I've learned a lot from this experience, and I plan to use those lessons from now on."

"You don't know how happy I am that I could be of some help to you. You don't need me for much. But I want you to need me. I need that, Darlene."

Why didn't I realize that? It never occurred to me, and all I've done is show him that I don't need him except to satisfy my libido. It's a lesson I won't forget, she thought. She saw a big replica of an ice-cream cone on top of a building that she'd passed most of her life. She had never been there before but decided to pull into the parking lot.

"Are we going in for ice cream?" he asked.

"If you want to, but I drove in here so I could put my arms around you. Why do you think I don't need you?" She turned to him, opening her arms as she did so. "I could hardly live through this week without you. You've changed my life, and I'm happy. When you're holding my hand, the stress melts away. I can't even describe it. I guess I mean that when I'm with you, whether walking side-by-side, in the kitchen, my office or in bed, I'm a whole person. I'm not the clinging-vine type, Mike. But I need you."

He tightened his grip on her, bent his head and brushed his lips over her mouth, eyes, nose and cheeks. "You're precious to me, Darlene. Don't forget that."

She kissed his nose. "I'd better get moving before I get a ticket for making out in public."

"Don't worry about that, sweetheart. I'll show him

my badge and get some respect. Did I tell you I've been promoted to chief of detectives?"

"No, you didn't. Congratulations. We'll drink to that when we get home. What does the chief do? Does it mean you'll be exposed to greater danger?"

"No. If anything, it will be less dangerous. Please don't worry about that."

She didn't want him to know it, but she did worry. "Here we are," she said.

Maggie met them at the door. "How are you two doing? I was on my way up the stairs when I saw your lights. Maybe you better put the car in the garage. According to the news, a storm's heading this way, and it's supposed to be a humdinger."

Mike held out his hand for the car keys. "I'd say that's a good idea. What about the windows?"

"All these windows are storm windows, but we can nail things down tomorrow morning. Good night."

"Good night," they said in unison.

"Darlene, do you have matches, candles and flashlights?"

"In the pantry."

"Why don't you round those up while I put the car in the garage?"

When he returned, she gave him a flashlight, took one for herself and left the candles and matches on the dining-room table. "Let's sit in the living room for a while," she said. "We have to toast to your promotion."

"But only for a minute. I have a feeling that tomorrow

will be a difficult day. We'd better get some sleep." After a glass of Tia Maria, they climbed the steps with Mike's arms around Darlene's waist and her head against his shoulder. She told herself that she could do that every night for the rest of her life. "Darlene, do you think you could kiss me without going for broke?"

"I can try."

She raised her arms to him, and, in that second, before he touched her, she committed to him. Her lips trembled when they met his. And as if he sensed that she was totally vulnerable, his hands stroked her body gently, tenderly, while his lips cherished her mouth.

"Go to bed, baby, while I can still let you go."

"You're spoiling me, Maggie," Mike said at breakfast the next morning. He leaned against the straight-backed kitchen chair and drank his coffee. "I could eat a breakfast like this twice a day."

"Only the first one would be breakfast," Darlene said, reaching up and tweaking his nose.

"That's one thing you two can't argue 'bout," Maggie said, "and I bet you'll try. This weather looks pretty bad. I don't think you ought to go out in this storm."

"I thought I'd make some calls to report back what I've found out about Albert Frank."

She glared at him. He held his hands up as if to surrender. "You know I'm still a detective, honey. That means I have to report anything that might have some bearing on my case."

White heat radiated from Darlene, and she seemed to

fume until he thought she'd explode. "How dare you?" she said, her voice trembling and her body shaking.

The doorbell rang, and neither of them moved, but sat staring at each other. Maggie got up. "Try not to kill each other before I get back." He couldn't remember a time in their relationship when Darlene had been so angry at him.

"I was on my way to Boonsboro and stopped to make sure that Darlene and Maggie were okay," Clark said. "Looks as if I barely beat the storm. We'd better shore up this place."

Mike stood and greeted Clark. "I'll help you. What can we expect?"

"Hurricane-strength wind, and it's heading here with nearly eighty-mile-an-hour winds."

After securing the storm windows and doors, the four of them repaired to the basement, where Maggie knitted and the others played pinochle.

The howling wind grew louder and louder. Through the cracks of light visible from the boarded-up basement window, they could see that the sky had darkened to night. Sounds of metal crashing and objects being tossed about sent chills through all of them. Mike looked at Darlene, her shoulders shivered in fright.

Suddenly, everything went black and the house shook violently. Mike sprang up, grabbed Darlene, rushed her under the pool table and covered her with his body. "I'll keep you safe," he whispered, "no matter what. You're my only love, everything to me."

She had barely breathed, but he felt her relax then

and slip her arms around him. "I know you care for me, and I'm not going to be angry with you. I do need you. I'm just frustrated."

"It's all right. We'll deal with that after the storm passes."

Nature's fury abated as suddenly as it began. Mike pulled himself and Darlene from under the pool table and held her for a few seconds, not caring about the eyes that watched him cherish her.

"Let's check out the damage, Clark. I hope it's only minor."

Chapter 6

Darlene went to the living room, sat down and attempted to collect her thoughts and retrieve her emotional balance. Maggie strolled to the kitchen casually, as if the storm had been just a calm, southern breeze. Darlene didn't care about what Clark and Mike would discover as they went through the house and searched outside it. Mike had shocked her more than the storm had. He'd showed her in the presence of her family that, if need be, he would protect her with his life. And then, he'd told her that he loved her. She tried to internalize it, to make sense of his feelings and hers.

"I'll have someone remove the tree limbs and replace the garage door. That's about it," she heard Clark say to Maggie when he and Mike came inside.

Maggie came into the living room with coffee and cake. "I thought for sure the wind was gonna take the roof off this house. Hmm, y'all sure are quiet."

Clark hugged Maggie and Darlene, finished his coffee and cake and stood. "I'd better get on to Boonsboro. It's been good to see you, Mike."

Maggie walked over to where Mike and Darlene sat together and refreshed their coffee cups. "I've been thinking 'bout how you'd feel if one of you had gotten hurt or worse during that storm. Life never guarantees you anything. You have a blessing in each other. So cherish it. If you don't stop arguing about unimportant things, you'll destroy God's gift."

Darlene loved Maggie, but she did not want a lecture, not on any topic. "I've had enough for today, Maggie."

Mike took her hand. "Let's walk outside for a while. Sometimes being in the open air clears the head." With his arm around her, they walked down the street for nearly half a block, seeing more evidence of nature's rage.

"What's that?" Darlene asked with a sound of terror in her voice.

"Some kind of… It could be a tornado. I don't like it. We'd better head back."

She had never associated fear with him, but she heard it in his voice. Knowing that he wanted to shield her from harm, she made herself smile as they walked faster and faster. Inside the house, he cradled her in his arms.

"I love you, Darlene, and I want us to pull together. I'll always be here for you, no matter what or where. Let's see if we can build a life together."

"I want that, too, Mike."

"But?"

"There aren't any buts. Promise me you will remember that as long as I practice law with Myrtle and Coppersmith, I'm a lawyer, and I'm required to consult with my partners on certain decisions. That doesn't mean I won't need your help sometimes. I will, but let me ask you for it when I need it."

"That makes sense."

The sun appeared, and with no evidence of another approaching storm, Darlene relaxed. "Now that I've completed my report, I'm going to drop it by the office, since it was due yesterday. I suspect Sam is there. Will you come with me? It won't take more than five minutes."

"Thank you for asking. Of course I will."

"Well, well," Sam said when he met them in the hallway. "That was some storm."

"Yes, it was. You remember Detective Raines?" The two men shook hands. "I thought I'd drop by and put the report on your desk."

She handed it to Sam, but it annoyed her that he began reading it while standing there. "Come on in the office." She followed Sam, but she held Mike's hand to let him know that she wanted him with her. "This is what we need, Darlene. I've begun to trust your judgment. I've defended clients who I suspected were guilty, but not one whose guilt I was certain of."

"I'm not going to defend him," Darlene said, her tone sharp.

"I agree. I have a case for you that you'll love." From her peripheral vision, she saw Mike sit forward. Alert. But whatever he wanted to say, he withheld his comments.

"What is it about?"

"A man who walked off the job because of unsafe working conditions. He got fired. The unions are behind him."

"That's for me," she said. "Thanks, Sam. I'll see you Monday. The day is half over, and Mike and I have a lot to do."

Mike shook hands with Sam Myrtle and left the office with her arm in arm.

"That case sounds a lot more interesting," he said. "If I were in your place, I'd consider it a real opportunity."

"Isn't it? I'm so glad it worked out this way. How would you like to visit some of our local wineries? Or, say, do you like antiques? We have some wonderful antique dealers. And Gettysburg is only thirty-three miles from here. What would you like to do?"

"If you want the truth, I'd love a shaded park bench, a hot dog and a cup of coffee."

"I know just the places for both." He didn't intervene during her talk with Sam, she mused, but he was there for her, and she didn't need more.

After consuming hot dogs and coffee, they sat

beneath a shading tree for nearly an hour, holding hands and hardly talking. "This past hour has meant far more to me than any sightseeing," he told her. "We need moments like this when we're comfortable with each other, just being together."

"Are you going back to Memphis tomorrow without making love to me?" She wanted to bite her tongue, but it was out there, and, with no one else near, she couldn't claim that it wasn't she who had said it. His quiet had begun to irritate her, and then he starting laughing. "Let me in on what's funny, will you?"

He threw back his head and whooped. "There I was thinking about the peace and contentment of being with you, and damned if you weren't thinking about sex."

"Well, I never wanted it at all till you did your thing. Now I get it in dribbles. What do you want from me? If you teach a rabbit to enjoy lettuce, dammit, he wants lettuce." Mike shook with laughter until he began to hiccup, stood and fought to get his breath. "Serves you right," she said, pounding him in the back.

A passing cyclist stopped. "You all right, buddy?"

"Thanks, man," Mike said with effort. "I'm okay." He reached for her hand. "Come on, baby, and let's go home. I don't want to *do* anything. I just want us to be together."

After dinner, they played pinochle with Maggie until she announced that she was sleepy. "I'm going to bed," she said. "Nobody gon' tell me y'all can't find somethin' to do other than play cards with me. Waffles at eight in the morning, Mike. Good night."

* * *

"Even she knows we ought to be doing something else," Darlene said. "So I don't see why you think celibacy is the way to go when you're in Frederick."

"Since when have you been able to read my thoughts? Where is Maggie's room?"

"On the back side of the house over the garden, the southwest corner. We're on the northeast side. Why?"

"I wouldn't like your family to think that I don't value you, and I want Maggie to respect me. If you think I've enjoyed being saintly, I haven't, but what you and I need will have to wait until you come to Memphis. Suppose you visit me next weekend."

She seemed hesitant, and he couldn't understand why. "Would you have invited me to visit you even if we did make love before you leave here?"

What a question! From time to time he glimpsed in her a lack of self-confidence where he was concerned, but at other times she could be strident with him. He attempted to put her at ease. "Sweetheart, it's been in my mind that each weekend, I would either be here or you'd be in Memphis, and whether we made love has nothing to do with it."

She went over to him and sat on his knee. "I told you that I'm no match for you, Mike. I'm not sophisticated, and I don't know how to be cool with men. I'll visit you next weekend, because I'm happy when we're together, and I…I'm at loose ends when you're there and I'm here."

"Get this straight, sweetheart. I want you right

now just as badly as I want to continue breathing, and controlling it is not easy. But you and I need to experience each other in ways other than sexually if we're going anywhere."

She jumped up. "Come on, let's check the door, douse the lights and go to bed before I change my mind and ravish you."

"Girl after my own heart."

He walked into his elegant condominium apartment at five o'clock Sunday afternoon, dropped his bag and went to the kitchen for a bottle of beer. But once there, he realized that he didn't want any beer. He wanted Darlene. Out of sorts and unwilling to try not to succumb to the mood, Mike got into his car and drove to Boyd's house. He didn't have a buddy, because his job made it difficult to cultivate close personal relationships. Boyd neither asked nor expected anything of him, merely accepted such measures of friendship as he offered.

Boyd, who was still under police protection until the trial, opened the door. His faced lit up with a warm smile. "How are you, Mike. If I'd known you were coming, I would have ordered some food for you. You brought dinner last time."

"Don't let that bother you. I just dropped by to see how you are."

"Never been better. Say, do you play chess? If you don't, I can teach you."

Mike's eyebrows shot up. It was an opportunity that he'd been waiting for. "Right, friend. I'd love a game."

After Boyd's first several moves, Mike looked hard at the man. "When I took the job of protecting you, I was told that your family might want to harm you. But I've never believed it. What's going on, Boyd?"

"You're being careful, because you don't want to upset me. Until I testify, my family stands to profit from those who don't want me to testify. They don't know that I'm on to them."

"Well, I'll be damned. The way you made those chess moves a minute ago, I figured you weren't as naive as I thought."

"How's Darlene?"

"We're getting along."

"Getting along? Considering where you were when she left here, by now you ought to be more than just getting along. You young fellows move at snail's pace. Don't you pussyfoot around and let Darlene get away. She's a wonderful person, and she cares a lot for you. Besides, she's beautiful."

"I know all that, Boyd. She's also got a short fuse."

"This is true, and yours is shorter."

"Yeah. That's what she says."

Boyd took a cell phone out of his shirt pocket. "I want a club-steak dinner and apple pie à la mode for desert. What do you want?"

Mike couldn't help shaking his head in amazement. "You're a load of surprises, Boyd. When did you get that fancy phone?"

Boyd allowed himself an elaborate shrug. "A couple

of days after they went on sale. I had it when we met. What should I order for you?"

Mike told him and added, "If you've got any more surprises, let me know them now."

Boyd's left eye closed in a meaningful wink. "There's more, friend, and you'll learn it in due time."

When she saw Mike waiting for her at the baggage carousel in Memphis International Airport, Darlene grabbed her chest in an effort to slow the pounding of her heart and quickened her stride. He didn't see her, and she sneaked up behind him and eased her arms around his waist.

"Whoever you're waiting for is out of luck, handsome. You're coming with me," she said.

He whirled around to face her, and a smile seemed to burst out of him. "You bet I am," he said, leaned down and flicked his tongue over the seams of her lips. "You're one fresh woman. I'll deal with you later." He lifted her bag from the carousel, took her hand and headed for his car.

"I reserved a room for you at the Peabody, but you may stay with me if you like. I have a guest room. It's up to you."

She had assumed that she'd stay with him, but at the moment she saw the disadvantage in that. Yet she didn't want him to feel as if she had rejected him. "I'll stay with you," she said, "and if you make me mad, I'll go stay with Boyd. Have you seen him recently?"

He put her bag into the trunk of his sedan, opened

the passenger door for her and failed to smother the grin that spread over his face. "Try not to lull me into complacency, sweetheart. Are you sure I met the right woman?"

"What does that mean?" She didn't try to control the iciness in her voice.

"This is the first time you've waited patiently until I got here to open the door for you." When her chin went up, he laughed, and she knew he expected her to try and have the last word. She didn't disappoint him.

"Maybe this is the first time you didn't take all day to get around here."

He reached over and tweaked her nose. "Now I know I've got my Darlene."

She eased down and rested her head against the back of the leather seat. "Did you tell Boyd I'd be here this weekend?"

"Actually, I didn't. After his lecture about not letting you get away from me, I decided he'd know when he saw you."

"He'll get a surprise. I brought him a harmonica."

"Why do you think he can play it?"

"I saw one in his house, but it was a cheap one. I bought him a Hohner Super 64 Chromonica harmonica. It's a really nice one, and I hope he likes it."

He pulled down the sun visor and turned the car onto Shelby Drive. "Darlene, I'm thirty-four years old, healthy and vigorous, and I will not let myself become jealous of a seventy-two-year-old man who lives alone and seems to enjoy it. What did you bring *me?*"

Her laughter had the sound of bells chiming in a soft breeze. "Silly. I brought you me."

He was not going to touch that one. "And what a gift. How's Maggie? Did she have anything to say about your spending a weekend with me?"

She seemed a little uneasy, and that perplexed him. He'd thought Maggie was in his camp. "Did you tell her?"

"Of course I did. She said that in matters such as these, chances are that the more a woman gives, the less she gets. Then she told me that it's always best to be honest and truthful."

"Hmm. I hope you've learned that I don't want to take advantage of you."

"I sure have. And I told Maggie that you're the one who's Saint Celibacy, not me."

He pulled over to the shoulder of Shelby Drive and gave in to the amusement that bubbled up and threatened to envelop him. Life with Darlene would definitely not be boring. "I can imagine her response to that."

"No, you can't. She said a man has a right to defend himself."

His cell phone rang before he could answer her. "Raines speaking."

"This is Detective Crawford. Your prisoner has decided to talk, but only to you. I know it's Friday, and you're off, but I need you here. You have to interrogate the guy."

Mike wanted to shout that the love of his life had just arrived and that he needed to be with her. "Look, man, I'm coming in from the airport with my weekend guest, who just arrived." He put his hand over the phone and related the problem to Darlene.

"Tell him not to keep you too long, because a warm and loving woman will be waiting for you."

He told himself to keep it between the lines, turned onto Elvis Presley Boulevard and headed home. "I'll be there within the next two hours, but I won't stay a minute beyond seven o'clock. And, buddy, you owe me a big one." He hung up and said to Darlene, "What do you want to do while I'm at the precinct?"

She rimmed her lips with the tip of her tongue. "Soak in a tub filled with warm bubbles."

"Darlene!"

"Okay. Okay. I'll be…uh…waiting for you."

Desire slammed into him. For every day of the past week, he'd been like a tomcat in an alley full of spayed females, ready to explode and with nothing to satisfy him. And now this!

"Cut me some slack. I definitely did not plan *this*."

"I know you didn't, hon. Get home as quickly as you can. If you're delayed, call me. I brought my cell."

"We're having dinner together tonight, no matter what kind of trick the suspect tries to pull." He opened his front door and stopped himself as he was about to lift her and carry her across the threshold in his arms.

"Come in," he said softly. "This is where I live."

She glanced up at him, but avoided eye contact. "Thanks for bringing me to your home, Mike."

"I'm sorry that you'll have to explore the place without me, but I've got barely enough time to get to the precinct."

She reached up and pressed a quick kiss to his lips, stirring him in a way that she could not have guessed. "You do what you have to do. I'll be here when you get home." She still hadn't looked him squarely in the face, and as bold as she could be, that didn't sit well with him.

"What's wrong, Darlene? What's the matter? Why can't you look at me?"

"I'm okay. I guess I'm just having a moment of immaturity."

He ran his fingers over his hair and shook his head. What had gotten into this normally sassy female? He stepped close and embraced her. "Are you sorry you came here?"

"No. I…I've never visited a guy…. I mean, stayed in his house. What's the protocol?"

He held her close and stroked her back. "Be your normal, wonderful self. If anything happens between us, you'll be the one to initiate it."

Her eyes sparkled, and he could see her wickedness overcoming her shyness. "You may be sorry you said that."

He let the laughter flow out of him, relieving his anxiety, not to speak of the tension. "Don't bet on it. If you're hungry, imagine how starved *I* am. And if you're not, I know what to dangle in front of you."

"What do you mean?" This time, she looked him in the face and narrowed her right eye.

"Lettuce, baby. I'm going to keep this little rabbit full of lettuce."

"Lettuce? Are you rowing with both oars? Oops!" She laughed. "Forget I said that."

"I never forget. I've been called a lot of things, but lettuce?" He glanced at his watch. "I'd better get out of here." He grasped her right hand, lifted her suitcase and led her up the stairs. "This is your room, Darlene. Stay sweet."

"You do the same."

What was she going to do with herself for the next three hours? A plan formed in her mind. She could at least have some fun. She heard the door shut and dialed his cell phone number.

"Raines. Darlene, what is it?"

"The minute you step out of that precinct, before you get in your car, call me on my cell. Okay? Don't forget. See you later."

"Sure thing."

A search of his refrigerator revealed nothing of interest. She went into his den, found the telephone book and got busy. Forty-five minutes later she paid one deliveryman for an assortment of delicacies, including crab salad, smoked sturgeon, artichokes, olives, slices of ham, cheeses and Italian bread. She paid another delivery person for a bottle of Grey Goose vodka, a bottle of dry vermouth and two bottles of white burgundy wine. She made a small ham sandwich and put it on the dining-room table along with a three-ounce glass of V8 juice that she found in the refrigerator. She stored the liquors in the refrigerator, arranged the meats and salads on a tray and placed them in the refrigerator. The bread and cheeses were left on a counter in the kitchen.

"I'm going to see what this brother is made of," she said to herself, took a tablet of paper from his desk and got busy. With her plans under control, she filled the tub in the bathroom with warm water and crystals the scent of which matched her perfume. Then she stripped and got in the tub. She'd never felt so wicked and downright decadent, and she luxuriated in the sinful feeling that the bath and her plans gave her.

Mike did his best with the job at hand, but as he probed the suspect for information, he could barely concentrate on the interrogation, for his thoughts were on what awaited him at home. And little did he know. At a quarter of seven, he left the precinct and gave silent thanks that he remembered to call Darlene.

"Hi, I'm sorry I had to leave you, but I'll see you in twenty minutes."

"Make it a short one," she said.

He managed to drive home without having an accident or getting a speeding ticket. "What's this?"

He stared at the large sign taped to the wall beside the foyer closet.

"FOLLOW THESE INSTRUCTIONS PRECISELY, AND YOU WILL BE A HAPPY MAN. Number one. Eat the small sandwich and drink the tomato juice on the dining-room table." Anxious for all the happiness he could get, he ate the sandwich and drank the juice. Beside the plate, he saw a folded piece of paper.

"Number two. Take off all your clothes and enjoy a nice warm shower. Then slip on your lovely gray cashmere robe."

Enjoying the game, he looked around for the next note and found it taped to the back of the bathroom door. Feeling warm and relaxed after the shower, he slipped on the robe and opened his next instruction.

"Number three. Go to your den, sit down and have a nice, soothing drink. No need to put on your shoes." He told his libido to take a nap.

He sat down at his desk, looked at the martini and grinned. She'd made certain that it would be cold, for she'd nestled it in a bowl of ice. He sipped it slowly, savoring it as one would any fine drink. "If she doesn't finish this game soon," he said aloud, "I'll be out of my mind and ready to explode."

He finished the drink and lifted the envelope beside it. "Don't open this until you've finished your drink and you're feeling mellow," the envelope said.

He was mellow, all right. With shaky fingers, he slit it open and read. "I'm in my room. Don't bother to knock." Desire slammed into him, and, try though he did to stave it off, his erection came swift, full and hard. After making certain that his robe was securely fastened, he strode the few paces to her room and was about to knock, when he remembered not to spoil the fun. He stepped in and gasped. She lay on the bed in what looked to him like a red jersey jumpsuit that was open almost to her navel. He saw the sides of her breasts, and liquid accumulated in his mouth. Speechless, he could only stare.

"Come here," she said, turning so that he saw most of one globe except the nipple.

He stumbled to the edge of the bed. For once, he had a willing woman in bed and was forced to wait for her move. "Come closer," she said, and when he leaned toward her, she reached out and fondled him.

"Hmm. Some goodies for me." She half whispered it. He bent forward to kiss her, and she turned so that her nipple glistened inches from his hungry mouth. She cupped it with both hands. "It's been itching ever since you called me. Don't you plan to drop that robe?"

He let it fall to the floor, pulled her up to him and claimed what she wanted him to have, fastened his lips on that turgid nipple and suckled voraciously. Sweet. She tasted so sweet. He slid his right hand down to her belly and got no farther, for her soft hands began to stroke and squeeze him, gently scratching his testicles.

"Let me taste," she said, then slipped down and sucked him into her mouth.

"Oh, my," he moaned. "Stop it! Stop it or I'll lose it."

"Sorry," she said, falling over on her back and licking

her lips. "You were taking so long. I thought I'd help you out."

"Yeah. I'll bet," he said, fighting to get his breath.

From the expression on his face, she wondered if she should grab her shoes and run. He had the look of a starved man who saw food within reach. Her panic must have shown on her face, for he pulled her to him with great care, as if he thought her fragile.

"Don't be afraid, sweetheart. I love you as you are. All you've done is whet my appetite. Kiss me. I need to know you care."

She parted her lips, pulled his tongue into her mouth and sucked. His hands moved over her body, hot, possessive and wild. When she felt his hard, hot sex against her thigh, her body shifted to him, and she could almost feel her blood begin its race to her loins. His lips teased her neck, and his tongue swirled in her ear.

She began to squirm. "You know what I want, and you won't give it to me."

"What? Tell me. I'll do anything you want. Anything! Tell me." She grabbed his thigh in an effort to pull him on top of her, but he didn't budge. His hands skimmed the inside of her thighs until she trapped them. "What do you want, baby?"

"I want… I want my nipple in your mouth."

He sucked on her nipple, pulling, teasing it with the tip of his tongue until the pulsating began in her vagina. "Is it good? Do you like it?" he asked, kissing his way down to her belly, where he lingered long enough to make her hips sway.

"Honey, please. You're playing with me. I want you to get into me."

"I will. Give yourself to me. Let me have you the way I want you." He spread her legs and rubbed her clitoris until she began to thrash, moving her head from side to side. Why couldn't it come? She wanted it so badly. "Mike. Honey, I'll die if I don't have it. Please get in me."

He raised her knees, bent to her and let her feel the thrust of his tongue. She screamed from the pleasure of it. And then he began to suck, nip and kiss alternately, bringing her to the brink and then letting the feeling go, until she thought she'd go mad.

"Get in me, Mike. Honey, I can't stand it."

He kissed his way up her body, and when he lay above her, looking down into her face, he smiled, electrifying her. She reached down, took his penis into her hands, raised her hips and felt him sink into her.

"Yes. Oh, yes," she said as he began to move.

"Come with me, baby," he said, and she knew it wouldn't last long. He unleashed his power, giving it to her in short, hard thrusts, and, immediately, the swell of heat began at the bottom of her feet.

"Don't strain for it, baby," he whispered. "We can't miss."

He put an arm beneath her hips, his other one around her shoulder, and began to storm within her, sending waves of sensation crashing through her vagina. She heard herself moan in frustration. Her thighs quivered out of control, and the swell settled in her vagina, pumping and squeezing until she cried aloud.

"Honey, help me. I…I'm dying. Oh, Mike. I love you. I love you so!"

Her vagina trapped him, squeezing and clutching him. "You're mine. Mine. Only mine," he cried out and fell into her arms.

She threw her arms wide, totally spent and happier than she'd ever been in her life. After about ten minutes during which she felt lifeless, she managed to lock her arms around him and squeeze him to her.

"Mike, please don't let me wake up and find that I've been dreaming."

"You aren't. This is us, sweetheart. You and me. And if we stay true to what we feel, nothing can ever separate us." He levered himself on his elbows, gazed down at her and grinned. "You did one hell of a job on me, woman. By the time I got to you, I was so fired up that I thought I was going to disappoint both of us. How'd you ever think up that scenario?"

"I was wondering what I'd do for almost four hours. Then I asked myself what I could do to make certain that you didn't take me to visit Boyd, then to a long, drawn-out dinner and finally bring me home and act the perfect gentleman, leaving it to me to make the first move. I figured that if it was up to me, I'd better leave no stone unturned."

"It was a clever scheme, and I enjoyed every second of it. I know you have a wicked streak that is always close to the surface, but this was more creative than devilish. Where'd you get the liquor and wine?"

"I found a telephone directory and had it delivered."

"I sure hope you ordered more than one ham sandwich."

"I did. Would you hand me that red robe in the closet."

"You mean you're planning to hide this perfect body from me?" His hands caressed her buttocks. "I didn't get a good look."

"You were doing what you had to do, and trust me, love, you did it expertly," she said.

He rolled out of the bed and strode proudly naked to the closet. "Keep talking to me like this, and I'll have such a big head that you won't be able to stand me."

"Not to worry. I'd help you keep your feet on the ground."

"Sure. Every woman knows how to do that," he said, helping her into the robe.

She didn't like his tone when he said it. "I don't want to get into anything that's unpleasant. I'm happy, and I want to stay that way. Let's go to the kitchen, so I can feed you." The two of them headed downstairs.

"Feed me what? There's nothing here except something for breakfast. I thought we'd eat out."

She put a finger to his lips. "Shh. I always heard that a man won't make love when he's hungry, and that afterward, he wants to eat. Set the table in the kitchen, and we can eat in ten minutes." She put the tray of food and the cheese on the table, sliced the bread and looked around for glasses. "There's a bottle of wine and a pitcher of martinis in the refrigerator," she told him and sat down.

"You're resourceful. I like that," he said. He opened the wine, put stem glasses at their places and poured a martini for himself. "Would you like a martini?"

She puckered her nose. "If I drank that, I'd be useless for the rest of the night. No, thanks."

Mike hooted. "Thanks for the warning that I'd better stay good and sober. I wouldn't exchange you for all the gold in Fort Knox." After saying grace, he ate some crab salad. "This is wonderful. When did you do all this?"

"Four hours is plenty of time for something like this. I knew I wasn't going to let you take me out of this house tonight, so that meant getting us some food."

"I'd have done that."

"Sure, but in that case, the evening wouldn't have gone as I wanted. I don't believe in leaving anything important to chance. Are you planning to visit me next weekend?"

"Sure, if you want me to. This is great cheese. In fact, this is a lot of food for two people. You planning to give me a workout?"

She looked at him from beneath the long, lowered lashes that swept her cheeks. "Would I do something like that?"

"Damn right you would, and I intend to see that you get the chance."

Chapter 7

Darlene sniffed the fragrant air. Coffee? Maggie must have changed from her regular… Something brushed her cheek, and when she attempted to knock it aside, it captured her mouth. Her eyes flew open.

"Mike! What on earth! Oh."

"Don't tell me you've forgotten that you spent the night in my arms." His lips brushed her forehead. "Drink this and come downstairs. Breakfast will be ready in twenty minutes."

She sipped the coffee, looked at him and smiled. "I could get used to you. What time is it?"

"Seven-thirty. I have a full day and evening planned for us."

"*Seven-thirty?* You'd make a great prison guard. What should I put on?"

"It's too cool for shorts, so some kind of pants or jeans would do it. I thought we'd go over to Meeman-Shelby Forest State Park, rent some bicycles and explore the trails. That park has some wonderful lakes, so we could go boating, if you like. We can visit Boyd at lunchtime, come back here and rest awhile, then make an evening of it. Did you bring something dressy?" She nodded. "Good. Get a move on, woman," he said and left the room whistling.

Darlene dragged herself out of bed, stretched and looked at the pillow beside the one on which she had slept. Yes, she had really spent a night in bed with a man. She remembered that his hand had rested beneath her breasts, and that he'd fondled them occasionally as he slept. She hugged herself and skipped to the bathroom. After taking a shower, she dressed in a yellow striped cotton shirt, jeans and a pair of Reeboks and managed to get to the kitchen in twenty minutes.

"You're a woman dear to my heart," he said. "One of the reasons is your punctuality. You don't keep me waiting. I have orange juice, fresh sweet raspberries or fresh pineapple. What is your pleasure, madam? Hmm. You look great first thing in the morning. I could definitely get used to you," he added, repeating her words to him earlier.

"What do I get in addition to fruit?"

"That's a loaded question, baby. In the event that you mean food, you can have scrambled eggs, toast, sausage and grits."

"I meant food. And I'll have all that and some raspberries. Thank you."

"You wound me. I can give you all that and me, too."

"Sex doesn't go with breakfast," she replied, her manner playfully haughty.

"Don't you fool yourself. Sex goes with *everything*."

She gaped at him. "Really? You've had sex while you ate? That's unbelievable."

"Cognac goes with a gourmet meal, but you don't drink it until you've finished eating."

"Very clever."

She finished what she regarded as a delicious breakfast, drained her coffee cup and looked at him with one eye closed. "Your wife won't need to know how to cook. You're perfect at it."

He leaned back and let his gaze travel over her. "That so? I guess I could handle that, provided she didn't mind getting up all times of night with our newborn babies and changing all the diapers. You know what I'm saying? Of course, if we went fifty-fifty with those things, I'd do whatever needed to be done."

"You can't carry a baby nine months," she said, not quite certain that she liked his reasoning, because she disliked cooking.

When he sat forward, she realized that they were having a serious discussion. He strummed his long, tapered fingers on the table. "No, I can't, Darlene, but I can carry *her* for the nine months and for the remainder of our lives, and I'd do it gladly and happily."

She reached over and stroked his hand. "I didn't mean for this to be a serious discussion. I was half-flippant, because I'm not crazy about cooking, although I'm not bad at it. Let's move on."

"Fine, but I was one hundred percent serious."

"I know you were. I'll do the dishes."

Laughter poured out of him, and she welcomed it. "You're a quick study," he said, "but I'll do it. By the time you get a jacket or a heavy sweater, I'll have finished. Ten minutes?"

"Eleven. I have to brush my teeth."

She'd wandered into that conversation unprepared, but she'd learned something about him, and it was something she should already have grasped. Michael Raines would take care of his wife and his children just as he did his work, leaving no stone unturned. And she'd learned another thing—when it came to his future as a family man, he did not have a sense of humor.

Ten minutes later, she met him at the bottom of the stairs wearing a burnt orange cardigan. "Won't I get too warm pedaling a bike in this sweater?"

Mike buttoned her sweater and belted it. "If so, you can tie it around your waist. I think you'll be comfortable, because it's only sixty-five degrees."

He put a long, woolen scarf around her neck. "Let's go. I want to kiss you so badly, but if I do, I know I won't want to stop."

She reached up, kissed him on the mouth and rushed

to the door. "That wasn't a kiss," she called over her shoulder.

"No, it wasn't. It was a tease."

At the park's general store, Mike parked his car and rented bicycles and helmets for them. "How long has it been since you rode a bike?" he asked Darlene.

"Oh, about three months. I can hold my own."

He bought some candy bars, along with two thermos bottles, which he filled with coffee. Then he smiled. "Who knows? You may get hungry."

"After that breakfast you fed me?" Suddenly, something flashed in her eyes that he hadn't seen in them before, and her lips quivered as she spoke. "You're a wonderful human being. You…you're such a sweet man. I could…"

"You could what?"

"A lot of things. Let's go."

At times, she could be so bold, and at others, she was as shy as a small child. He wanted to hug her close to him and protect her from everything, but he restrained himself, fought back the emotion that washed over him like a mammoth ocean wave and draped an arm loosely across her shoulder. Outside of the store, she donned the helmet, and he fastened it beneath her chin. Then he watched while she swung onto the bike like a champion racer, got on his own and guided her toward his favorite trail.

Autumn had already begun to change the colors in nature. They rode along a winding bicycle path into the deep woods, woods now resplendent in yellow, orange, brown, red and green. He hadn't thought that they would find such beauty, for he usually rode there in spring and midsummer.

"This is spectacular," she said. "Thank you so much for bringing me here. It's breathtaking."

It pleased him that they could enjoy nature together. "We're very near the lake. Shall we go over there? We'll have to walk our bikes."

"Yes. I'd love to see the reflection of these trees in the lake. What's that?"

"The fish are jumping. We can't fish because we don't have a license."

"I love to fish in the Monocacy River about three-quarters of a mile from our house. Next time I'm here, maybe we can fish."

"I'll get a license."

That look in her eyes again! He doubted that she was aware of whatever was going on there, but it would soon reveal itself. They leaned the bikes against a big oak tree and stood quietly as they feasted their eyes on the lake and its reflections of the forest.

Suddenly, she grasped his arm and, still gazing at the lake, said, "This place is like you."

He sucked in his breath. He would never have expected to hear any woman compare him to such beautiful scenery. "Thank you, but I think you're overstating it." Still, her words touched him deeply, and with his hands on her shoulders, he turned her to face him. "I'm just a man, Darlene, and I can and do make mistakes. Don't make me into something that I'm not and can't be."

She laid her head to the side and looked at him. Flirting. He shook his head as if to clear it. She was actually flirting with him in a public park owned by the state of Tennessee. Shivers plowed through him, and he pushed her away. If she touched him, he would explode. She knew that he wanted her like he wanted air to breathe, and he was damned if he'd be a victim of it. Oh, hell, maybe he was being unfair to her. He was about to suggest that they leave when she raised her head, lowered her lashes and ran her tongue over the seam of her lips.

Damn her! He picked her up and braced her against a big poplar tree. "You listen to me, Darlene. You told me last night that you love me, and you told me that half a dozen times, but always when we are having sex. Sex and love are not the same. Do you hear me? A man can have sex with a woman he doesn't give a damn about, and all he wants is physical relief.

"But *I* made love to you last night, woman, and it wasn't just a mere sexual experience. I gave you myself, my body, my heart, my whole being. Tell me you gave me the same." He winced at his words. *Good Lord! Had he gone too far?*

Tears streamed down her face, but she looked him in the eye. "I know you gave yourself to me, Mike. All of you, and that made me love you more. But do you know that you took just as much from me? Do you know that I am not and cannot ever again be the woman I was when

I awakened yesterday morning? You made me a part of you. I awakened this morning to your kiss, and I was so proud, not because I came to life in your arms, but because I was one with you. Do you understand what I'm trying to say?"

He did, and he told her so. Holding her closer, he said, "We're magic together. I want to capture in our daily lives what we find together in bed."

She let her fingers graze his beloved cheek. "Does that mean I have to like to cook?"

He parted his lips over hers, and when she pulled his tongue into her mouth and sucked it, he took what she gave him and allowed himself to be happy. "Nobody said you had to like it," he said with a wide grin.

"Oh! You!"

"Still love me?" he asked her.

"Is that a serious question? If it is, I'll let you know."

"You're being fresh again. What do you say we take the bikes back and do a little sightseeing in town?"

"I'd like that. I want to see the National Civil Rights Museum. Is it far from here?"

"Not too far. It's in the Lorraine Motel, where Dr. King was assassinated. There's also the Underground Railroad Museum, the Alex Haley Museum and several other notable places. This town is rich in the history of African-Americans. And don't forget Beale Street. The town fathers advertise that Memphis gave birth to the blues, but their reasons for appreciating it begin and end with tourism and the money it brings. At the Cotton Museum, you get the city's history from blues to sharecropping to the city as it is today, and you know who played and sang the blues and suffered the sharecropping. It's black history. Where shall we start?"

"What do you suggest?"

"Let's start with the Underground Railroad Museum. That Civil Rights Museum is depressing."

They returned the bikes and helmets, then sat on the porch of the general store while eating the chocolate bars and drinking the coffee. He bought for Darlene a small carving of an eighteenth-century trapper as a souvenir of their outing, and they were soon on their way to her first real dose of Southern history. She wasn't sure that she wanted to experience it, but she knew that if she did, she would be richer for it.

"We don't have half the guts that our forebears had. Imagine shivering in that secret cellar and going through that trapdoor not knowing what you'd find or who would find you," she said when they were leaving Slave Haven Underground Railroad Museum. "The desire for freedom must have been one powerful drug."

"Sure it was. Many of them lived in hell. It's too bad that our young people today don't appreciate what our ancestors suffered in their fights for freedom. Let's go home and change before we go to see Boyd. And none of your tricks, unless you don't want to see Boyd."

"I don't play tricks with you."

"Of course you don't. And the Mississippi River runs through the middle of New York City." He stopped for a red light, leaned over and kissed her. "But I wouldn't exchange you for anything." He turned into Beale Street and slowed down. "This is one of the most famous streets in the country. It comes alive at night."

"I'll bet it does." She turned to him. "Do you love living here?"

He did not love the city of Memphis. But something was behind that question, so he'd better answer as honestly as he could. "My work is here. It is here that I have roots, a reputation and the respected status that I worked hard to earn."

She patted his knee, leaned back against the leather seat and closed her eyes. He didn't know what that meant, but he hoped that his answer didn't unsettle her. If he was in luck, she'd be comfortable with it.

"I'm reluctant to tell a woman that she has forty-five minutes in which to get dressed, but can you…uh, manage to do that and be here in the foyer by a quarter past twelve?"

Her chin went up, and he prepared himself for some biting words. "That was a male-chauvinist remark. Of course I can. But if I had to put on an evening dress, it would be a different matter."

When he hugged her, she snuggled close, like a kitten in a blanket. She was soft and sweet like a kitten, too. "Do you like pets?" he asked her. "You ought to have a little kitten."

"I like them, but when they grow up, they're so ornery. Puppies are more dependable." She looked at her watch. "You have no mercy. Now I have only forty-three minutes."

He stared after her as she sped down the hall. Was he inching closer to giving up his cherished bachelorhood? Could she handle his frequent and sometimes long absences in connection with his work? He didn't know whether he was ready to risk that with her. But, Lord, she was so sweet and loving, and when he was deep inside of her, he barely knew who he was. He headed for his room and a shower, grateful that each bedroom had its own bath.

Shortly before they reached Boyd's house, his cell phone rang. "This is Crawford. Can you come down and give me about an hour."

Mike's laughter had the sound of a feral growl. "Man, you screwed up my date yesterday, but definitely not today. I'll see you Monday morning and not a minute before. If you've got any suspects, let 'em rest in the county jail for a while."

"But Mike, this one is clever, and he may have robbed a string of banks in the—"

"You want to ruin my life? No way, man. My dad always said that if you don't take care of your own business, nobody is going to do it for you. Would you ditch your wife in order to ask some guy why he took something out of a bank that he didn't put in there? No, you would not. See you." He hung up.

"I'm glad you told him no," Darlene said. "I don't think I could come up with a scenario that equaled last evening."

"You probably couldn't, but I wouldn't mind if you worked out something and kept it in reserve. Not knowing what a woman will do next keeps a man's engine revved and ready to run." He parked in front of the house, walked around the car and opened the door for Darlene.

"Thanks," she said. "I want you to know that I feel like a dummy sitting there, as if I'm too weak to open a door. I do it just to please you." She got out and looked up at him. "I need you in more meaningful ways, Mike, like this lost feeling I have when I'm not with you. I need your hand on me somewhere, so I'll know you're here, really here. If something's funny, I enjoy it more if we laugh about it together. And if I'm miserable, I want your arms around me." Suddenly, she grinned. "Sorry. I can't imagine what brought all that on."

She reached for the doorbell, but he stopped her. "For once, you gave it to me straight, exactly as you felt it, and it was motivated by your need for me to understand you, to know you deep down, and not by a plunge into an orgasmic vortex."

She looked past his shoulder. "We all have our moments of reckoning, Mike. Let's just say that was one of mine." She pushed the doorbell, and, seconds later, Boyd opened the door, his face alit with a broad grin.

"It's time you—"

"Darlene! Mike didn't tell me you were coming with him." He opened his arms, and she went into them as if she belonged there. He glared at Mike. "And here I was worrying, whether the two of you were getting together and working things out."

"Don't be hard on him, Boyd. Mike is straighter than the crow flies."

"I know that, and I'm glad to see that you come to his defense."

"Come on, you two," Mike said. "We're going to the Peabody Grill, unless one of you objects."

"I never object to eating good food," Boyd said. "It's the best Memphis has to offer. How about you, Darlene?"

"The Peabody Grill is wonderful. I'll be happy anyplace, as long as I'm with two of my favorite people."

"I'll get you for that," Mike said under his breath. "Expect to beg for mercy before you sleep."

As he'd hoped, she heard him. "Believe me, I can't wait. Make my punishment as hard as you like."

Mike sucked in his breath and fought back the devil libido. "You love to live dangerously, and one of these days, I'm going to accommodate you."

"We can have coffee and desert here later, if you have time," Boyd said. "I made a delicious peach pie with some peaches I froze in July, and I have some really good ice cream."

"Works for me," Darlene said. "I've already decided that I want pulled pork for lunch. And it's better here in Memphis than in any other place." She turned and looked back at Boyd. "Have you had any more break-ins?"

"Not a one. I think Mike solved that problem. The

fellow who tried to break in was hired by someone, but I'm not sure who."

"Yeah," Mike said. "The guy was a family man who'd been out of work for over two years. He had no criminal record. He pleaded guilty to a lesser charge, and when Boyd declined to press more serious charges, the man got three years' probation. I'm glad it's over."

"What about the man you're testifying against? Isn't he also a criminal?"

"Sure thing," Mike said. "He's going to spend a few years thinking about it while he makes license plates, or some such thing, as a guest of the state."

The maître d' rushed to them when they entered the room. "Right on time, as usual, Mr. Raines," the maître d' said. Then he recognized Boyd and all but genuflected. "Mr. Farmer! What a pleasure to see you. We heard that you haven't been well."

"Never been better, Marvin. When you're old and in good health, that doesn't sit well with some of your relatives. I hope your folks are more charitable." Boyd's eyes twinkled with mischief, leaving the maître d' speechless.

Mike looked from the maître d' to Boyd and decided that he was seeing his friend as he really was, and that the continual deference, even meekness, that he had observed in Boyd while he and his house were under police protection was indeed an act, and a skillful one at that.

"I don't know why you want to pay these awful prices," Boyd said to Mike as he regarded the three asparagus spears on his plate. "If you took Darlene and me to Burger King, we'd be happy, wouldn't we, Darlene?"

"Absolutely, as long as they didn't put any raw onions on the burger. But Mike wanted us to have a pleasant reunion, and, gentleman that he is, he's done it in style."

Boyd seemed for a minute to have sunk into the distant past. He shook his head very slowly. "Mike, if the woman I wanted had had the faith in me that Darlene has in you, and if she had defended me instead of tearing me down, there's no telling what I would have become."

Darlene and Mike stopped eating and stared at Boyd. "Not to worry," he said. "I've been over that for thirty-seven years. Well over it. Pricey or not, Mike, this steak is talking business. It's scrumptious."

"It can't possibly be better than my pulled-pork sandwich. It's wonderful."

They declined dessert, which they planned to enjoy at Boyd's home, and were soon headed there. Mike glanced quickly at his watch to be sure that he had time for everything that he'd planned for Darlene. As soon as they entered Boyd's house, he went with his friend to the kitchen.

"I'll make the coffee, Boyd. Nothing will convince me that since I was last here, four days ago, you've learned how to make coffee. It's as simple as measuring four cups of water and heaping this measuring gadget with coffee five times." He boiled the water and made the coffee. "Where's the dessert?"

"The pie's heating in the microwave oven. You scoop up some ice cream, and we—"

Mike let the laughter roll out of him. "Man, you're a genius at getting what you want. I forgot that you don't like to dip up ice cream, that it makes your hands cold. You're a piece of work. If I could, I'd adopt you."

"Who knows?" Boyd said, his eyes twinkling with mischief again. "You take care of Darlene. That's all I'm asking of you right now. Why are you making this such a short visit, Darlene?"

"I have to be in court Monday morning, so I should be at home tomorrow afternoon or evening at the latest to study my case and get some rest. A family is suing the builder of their house for fraud, because of shoddy work and for subcontracting, which their contract forbade."

A frown altered the contours of Mike's face. "I thought Sam gave you a case dealing with labor relations."

"He did, but I usually have two or three cases to work on. I should wrap this one up in a few days. The defendants want to settle out of court, and that would be a good thing, because the jury is not going to give my clients what they're asking for. No way."

"When will you come back to Memphis, Darlene? I want to talk seriously with the two of you," Boyd asked.

"It's hard to say, Boyd," Darlene said, her mind barely able to think beyond the weekend.

Consecutive weekends in Memphis? Did she want that or didn't she? And what was Boyd's motive? No one had to tell her that she should encourage Mike. She was crazy about him, and she was not a fool.

"I don't know, Boyd," she said, looking at Mike. "Depends on if and when I get an invitation."

"Can you come back next weekend?" Mike asked her. "I wouldn't mind if you didn't bother to go back, except that you have to work."

"You should visit me next weekend."

"Didn't I visit you on two consecutive weekends? But I'm also willing to visit you next weekend, if that would please you."

She looked at Boyd. "This guy plays dangerously."

"I know," Boyd said. "He's very good, but I beat him at chess." He softened his voice. "Darlene, don't you want to come here next weekend?"

"I do, but it doesn't matter whether he's there or I'm here. I want us to be together."

Mike stood. "We have to leave now. I'd be happy if you'd come here next weekend, Darlene. Will you?"

"Yes," she said, getting to her feet. "I sense some unfinished business here." She hugged Boyd. "It was wonderful to be with you. I hope to see you next weekend. Oh. I almost forgot." She took the small package from her handbag and handed Boyd the harmonica she'd bought for him.

His eyes widened. "For me? This is for me? Oh, thank you. I haven't had a present in years."

She kissed his cheek. "You're welcome. Bye."

* * *

Mike figured that Boyd had just spiked his plans. He didn't much mind, though, because it meant that he'd have Darlene with him the following weekend. But it meant a change of plans for the evening. He hoped she'd be agreeable to having a more casual evening than he'd originally planned. He seated her in his car, hooked her seat belt and grinned down at her.

"There've been a number of times when I wished you'd be less feisty, but I like the fire in you. Don't get docile on me, Darlene."

She looked at him wide-eyed, as if he had handed her a stunning surprise. "Me? Docile? One of us is dreaming."

He leaned over and brushed her cheek with his lips. "What do you think Boyd wants to talk with us about?"

"I'm afraid to guess. If he wants to talk to me about you, I'm ready to tell him what I think of people who meddle."

He certainly had not expected that. "I'd have a hard time telling Boyd to mind his business, no matter what he said to me. It would be tantamount to telling my father to bug off."

"I know. I have such affection for him, and that seems weird considering how little I know of him."

"Is your dress for this evening long or short?" Her answer would tell him which of his plans he had to cancel.

"It's a short one. It's dressy, but if I wear its jacket,

it will be good-looking and dance-worthy, but not good enough for a gala."

"Great. I thought we'd have a really nice dinner and then take in some jazz and dance."

"That suits me, Mike, and I know I'll enjoy it. Don't knock yourself out entertaining me. Sitting on a park bench with your arm around me can keep me happy for a good while."

"I appreciate that, Darlene, but I'm taking it with a grain of salt. You're never going to tell me that I don't take you anywhere."

Her laughter exploded out of her. "Whose parents have you been listening to?"

"Nobody's. But I work with a bunch of policemen, and that's one of their biggest gripes. When they get home after a rough day, they want to sit on the couch, drink a beer and watch *Law and Order*. And their wives complain that they never take them anywhere."

"Is that what you do? Chill out on the couch with a can of beer?"

He laughed aloud. "Not yet. I haven't sunk to that, and I hope I never will. I'm not a passive person. I'd rather make things happen than have them happen willy-nilly to me."

She cast a sidelong glance at him. "If you're tired, we can stay in this evening."

He parked the car in front of the building in which he lived and played that last sentence over and over in his mind. "If you're joking, I accept it, but if you're not, something's out of kilter. Which is it?"

She leaned back in the seat and looked straight at him. "You'd best learn to trust me, Mike. On the one hand, I was joking, but on the other, I'm prepared to go with your program. You know this place better than I do."

"You're always teasing," he said, "and there are times when I like to be sure."

She reached for his hand and snuggled closer to him. "What time are we leaving home?" He told her. "Hmm. A quarter of seven? That gives me plenty of time for a nice long bubble bath."

"Unless you want company in that tub, keep those thoughts to yourself. I have no interest in sainthood, so don't tempt me."

Her arm eased around his waist. "If I don't take it before I go, I don't think you'll give me a chance to enjoy one after we come back."

He held her, kissed her chin and got out of the car. He opened her door, unhooked her seat belt and looked down at her. "The only temptation Adam had was an apple, and look at what he started. Suppose he'd had to deal with you!"

Her right eye closed in a sexy wink. "I'll bet he wasn't a quarter of the man that you are." Having said that, she headed to the building's entrance, leaving him to follow her or not. What a princess! And what if he'd never met her? He inhaled a long, deep breath. Life was good, and he was blessed.

Darlene didn't want Mike to think that unless he spent money on her, she wouldn't he happy. She loved nice restaurants, fancy hotels and business-class accommodation on airplanes, but she didn't need any of it. Yet if she told him, he'd probably feel unappreciated. She lounged in the tub filled with warm lavender bubbles, stuck her toes out of the suds and admired her pedicure. She liked herself, but she would have been happier if she wore a size nine rather than a ten and a half. But most tall women had long feet, and she liked her height.

After half an hour, when the water began to cool, she got out, dried off, pampered her body with scented lotion, put on a yellow bra and bikini panties, and her kimono. She got the trial notes that she brought with her, sat up in bed and underlined the points that she wanted to emphasize. After studying her brief carefully, she put the notes aside, took out her phone and called Maggie. Mike wouldn't mind if she used his phone, but she considered that inappropriate. If she were engaged to him, she'd do it, but friendship didn't cover everything.

"Hi, Maggie. How are things?"

"It's time you called. I thought your plane was still circling the Memphis airport. You having a good time?"

"Absolutely. Mike is the most considerate person. We've been biking, sightseeing, visiting a friend, and now I'm resting."

"Mind if I ask where you're resting?"

"I'm in my room. Where else would I be?"

"Don't ask me. Sometimes you use sense and

sometimes you don't. I hope you're working on that relationship."

"Of course I am, Maggie. Why do you think I came here?"

"You didn't tell me, so I don't know. You coming home tomorrow?"

"Yes. My flight leaves around noon."

"Well, give him a hug for me." She said she would and hung up. Hopefully Maggie wouldn't get the wrong impression about her returning to Memphis the next weekend. She shrugged. *I can't let what people think govern my behavior,* she thought.

Her cell phone rang. "Hello?"

"Does the most beautiful girl in the world know that it's already six-thirty? It's so quiet, not even the sound of the radio, that I feared you were asleep."

"I've been wide-awake since you kissed me this morning. I'll see you at the foyer in fifteen minutes."

"Fourteen."

"All right. Fourteen it is. Now hang up so I can finish dressing. Kisses."

"Kisses to you, and from head to foot."

She hung up, but she tingled all over. That was exactly how he'd kiss her, and she hoped he wouldn't forget that when he brought her home.

She slipped on a yellow sleeveless silk dress that had a deep cowl neckline that made her breasts look ready to pop and had shirring from beneath them to the hem. She put on the short matching jacket, a pair of gold hoops, added a light coating of burnt orange lipstick, dabbed perfume where it counted and arrived at the foyer seconds before Mike did.

"Who is this gorgeous female?" He opened his arms and she walked into them and relaxed, as if finding shelter from a storm. "You make a man proud," he said as they got into his car. "I prefer the Peabody, but I thought we'd try McEwen's tonight. It's quiet and elegant, and the food is excellent."

"I am in your capable hands. You won't let us starve, because you subscribe to the theory that loving and starving don't go together."

"I also subscribe to the dictum that one does not say everything that one thinks."

She couldn't help laughing. "Mike, honey, if I did that, you'd have run the other way two hours after we met."

His eyes widened. "Really? What were you thinking? We're close, so you can tell me now."

"Yeah. Right. Oh, what the heck! I wondered what you'd be like in bed. Did you wonder about me?"

"You bet your beautiful tush I did, although you made me so mad that it was at least three hours before I got around to that." He parked at McEwen's, got out and helped Darlene.

"This looks like a mansion," she said, clearly awed.

The dim lights and flickering candles highlighted his features.

"In this light, you look like a dream. How is it that of all the men you've met, you love me? I can hardly fathom it. You're smart, accomplished, grounded and so beautiful. And you suit me in every way."

"What a nice thing for you to say to me, Mike. When I muse over the things about you that draw me to you, I wonder how it is that some clever woman didn't get you years ago. I don't know why I love you, but I know why you're so dear to me. I know you're there for me, and that you will always be there so long as we're together."

He held her hand and gazed into her eyes as the flickering candles cast their silhouettes on the wall. "Do I have the music that makes you dance?"

She lowered her gaze, because she couldn't handle the look that said I know you inside and out. "I gave you the answer to that question several times last night."

"Yes, you did. And I'll never get enough of it."

"Me, neither. Never."

Chapter 8

Darlene walked into court that Monday morning, put her briefcase on the table assigned to her and walked over to the opposing attorney, a formidable, older man of considerable reputation, to introduce herself. She extended her hand. He glanced at her and continued examining his papers.

A smile played around Darlene's lips, and she told herself not to laugh. "I'm delighted to meet you, D.A. Holmes. I'm Darlene Cunningham." The man stared at her with an expression that said when did she get the temerity to speak to him. After a moment, he quickly stood up, evidently remembering his status, and shook her hand.

"How do you do, Ms. Cunningham?" He hesitated.

"You're rather young for this case, aren't you? It'll be a rough one."

Enjoying the fact that she'd rattled him, at least for the moment, she spoke up again. "Young in age, perhaps, but not in ability. I'm sure this trial will be a memorable one."

Let him digest that!

Having drawn her sword, she went back to her table, satisfied that she had at least made the man cautious, hopefully sparing herself the spectacle of his courtroom antics and shenanigans. The morning went by quickly, and the judge recessed the trial until one-thirty.

After a lunch of two crab cakes and hot tea, she phoned Mike. "Hi, how'd the interrogation go this morning?"

"Useless, honey. Crawford could easily have done it. But he likes to think he's so tough that suspects see him as an adversary and won't talk to him."

"Is he? Worse than you, I mean?"

"Mind your mouth, woman. He's a pushover, and he knows it. You're in court?"

"Yes. I think I have a decent jury, though I've learned that one shouldn't count on that. Problem is that I'm facing one of the smartest corporate litigators in the whole of Frederick County."

"If you've done your homework, you needn't worry. Your client is innocent, his case is one that will inspire sympathy and you have good, credible witnesses."

"I know, and I'm not worried… Well, only a little. Dueling with Frank Holmes is no joke."

"It doesn't matter who you're up against."

"Yeah, but I'm not afraid of him. We'll see how it goes. My problem is having to wait until Friday to see you."

"I'm dealing with that, too. What time will the judge recess court on Friday?"

"Usually the courthouse shuts down on Fridays at noon. It's hard to believe that on one weekend, two short days, I got as accustomed to being with you as I did. Gotta finish my lunch and get back to court. Love ya."

"And I love you. I'll call you tonight."

The wrangling in court hadn't truly begun. Yet when she got home that night, she flopped down on the living-room sofa and spread her arms, exhausted. With everyone in the courtroom watching her every word and her adversary taking thorough notes, hours of courtroom drama had worn her out.

Maggie came into the living room with a cup of tea and handed it to Darlene. "What you doing in there? You all right?"

"Thanks. I'm more concerned with convincing the jury than I am about how tired I am."

Darlene sipped tea and shrugged. "I wonder why I can't seem to concentrate?"

"'Cause your head's full of Mike. How is he?"

"Wonderful. I'm going to treat my muscles to a hot shower. I'll be back down in about an hour."

After the hot shower, she felt much better. "Hello," she said, answering the phone in her room.

"Way to go, sis. I heard about your case this afternoon. Hearing about you, I asked myself what happened to my little sister. Apparently, you were really sharp in that courtroom."

"Thanks, Clark. I'm glad you think so. I decided today that a prerequisite for becoming a litigator should be at least two semesters in acting."

"That bad, huh? Things still working with Mike?"

"You could say that. I spoke with him this afternoon. What's going on with Tyra? Anything?"

"She's good. She takes to marriage and motherhood like a bird takes to the air. I'm happy for her. Andy practically worships her, and she adores him. When she married Byron, she made the right move, sis, and I hope you do as well."

"What about you and Caroline?"

"You know I move slowly. When it comes to relationships, that's the best policy." They talked for a while, and then she went down the stairs to eat dinner. From the time she and Mike made love in her bed, being in that room made her feel close to him, but it could also make her feel lonely.

"Let's rent a movie," she suggested to Maggie. "I need a distraction."

"You want to think about something other than your work, or other than Mike?'

"Other than work."

"Then you don't have to rent a movie. Phone him. He'll keep your mind occupied."

Darlene got up and turned on the television, not that she wanted to watch anything; she wanted to make the time pass. "I phoned him during my lunch hour. He said he'd call tonight, and he will."

"Then read something. You're giving my nerves a fit. Being in love never meant a woman had to go crazy."

"Come on, Maggie. I remember when you got married. You drove us nearly insane. You burned the food, didn't remember where you parked your car and forgot to buy groceries. You were a wreck. And on your wedding day, Clark practically led you to the altar, because you couldn't see through the tears that washed your face and soaked that lovely gown."

"Yes," Maggie said with longing and sadness. "I loved the ground he walked on. He's been gone twelve years, and for me, it's just this morning." She shook her head. "But I'd rather have had those years with him and the pain of his death than never to have had him. He was one awesome man."

Maggie wiped a tear, and the phone rang. Darlene raced up the stairs to take the call in her room, the place where she felt close to him.

A glance at her caller ID, and her heart began to race. "Hi."

"Hi, yourself. Have you been running?"

"I ran up the stairs because I didn't want to talk with you in front of Maggie."

"I don't have anything new to say to you. I called

because I needed to connect with you, and this is the best I can do."

"I know. I miss you, too."

"I'll be in Charlotte, North Carolina, tomorrow, but I'll be back here tomorrow night. If you need me, dial my cell number. How did the trial go this afternoon?"

"The attorney hasn't wrapped up its case yet, but they want to call a witness who is testifying for my client, and that tells me that their case is weaker than I thought."

"Perhaps, but don't be too confident."

"I appreciate what you're saying, and I know I have to guard against that. Justice isn't always served well."

"You're right. I have to get up at five to make a seven-forty flight, so I'll say good-night. I love you, sweetheart. Dream about me."

"I love you, too, hon. I can't promise to dream of you, because if I go to bed thinking about you, I may not get to sleep." She made the sound of a kiss. "I can't hang up until you do."

"You don't think I'm going to hang up on you, do you?" She heard the laughter in his voice, a sound like soft wind swirling in a deep valley.

"Okay. Let's hang up on the count of five. One…"

She rolled over on the bed, hugging a pillow to her body. With the feel of her nipples tightening, she fell over on her belly and moaned softly. She wasn't used to needing a man, and she wasn't sure she liked it. Oh, why did love have to be so complicated? She got ready for bed, crawled in and prayed that she would sleep.

Her career could depend on this case, since the jury's decision could affect workers throughout the country.

As she was leaving home for work the next morning, she met a delivery boy on the walk between the street and her house. "Does Darlene Cunningham live here?"

"I'm Darlene Cunningham."

"Would you sign for this?" he asked as he handed her a basket of tea roses.

She opened the envelope. "Just a minute," she said, remembering what Mike had warned her about before. She was not going to sign for something that she didn't want.

"Have a wonderful day, darling. Love, Mike." She signed for it, gave the boy a tip and went back inside, where she put the flowers on the dining-room table. He had a way of getting to her down deep where she lived. She loved flowers, and the tea roses' dusty rose color had long been her favorite. Her steps quickened, and not even the darkening clouds could daunt her spirit or rob her of the joy she felt. Frank Holmes might be a lion of a prosecutor but she could hold her own, and she'd bet nobody had sent him a basket filled with several dozen flowers. She laughed aloud as she parked near the courthouse.

"It's my day," she said to herself. "I've got the world by the tail."

Darlene questioned three witnesses that morning, and when the third one left the stand, she had to repress her relief and pleasure. Frank Holmes did not cross-examine him, and a long look at the noted trial lawyer told her that he was not expecting to win the case.

At lunchtime, she went to a tiny café a couple of blocks from the courthouse, ordered a tuna-fish sandwich and coffee and studied her notes. Her afternoon witness could prove difficult. She got back to the court ten minutes before trial time and learned that the corporate defendants were anxious to settle out of court. She and the plaintiff agreed, but she reserved the right to disclose the terms of the settlement.

"That's good enough," Sam told her. "They were getting a lot of bad publicity that was ruining their image. We'll see that this gets wide publicity. It's good for the plaintiff, and great for Myrtle, Coppersmith and Cunningham."

In her office that afternoon, Darlene called her older sister, Tyra, to let her know the outcome of the trial. "I hadn't expected that it would go so well, though I expected to win," she told Tyra.

"I caught part of it on the local news last night. Clark's right. You're really good. Little sis is a big girl now. Why don't you come over and have supper with us this evening?"

"Good idea. I haven't seen Andy for a while, and Maggie won't have to cook. I'll be there around six."

As she sat down to supper with Tyra, Andy, Byron and Jonie, Byron's aunt, the doorbell rang. Byron went to open the door and came back with Clark.

"Hi, everybody," Clark said after hugging Darlene. "Sorry I'm late, but the traffic is a killer ."

"It's all right, Uncle Clark," Andy said. "We haven't said grace yet. Uncle Clark, I've decided that everybody is going to call me Anthony. That's really my name, and I'm too old to be called Andy."

Clark took a seat at the table. "That's right, son. When I'm around you, I forget how old a five-year-old really is."

Darlene enjoyed being with her family, but she knew Mike would call her, and she didn't want to be with them if he called her on her cell phone. "I hate to run," she said at about eight-fifteen, "but I have to work tomorrow."

"You did a great job on that case," Byron said. "If you ever get tired of working for Myrtle and Coppersmith, you know where there's an opening."

"Thanks, Byron. I will seriously keep that in mind." She kissed each of them and was soon on her way home.

When she tuned in the ten o'clock local news, it stunned her to see her face on the screen and to hear herself referred to as a champion of the working man.

"Why?" Mike asked when she told him about it. "You can't imagine how proud I am of you. I'm going to have to do something about this calendar. There're seven days in a week, but Friday takes seven times as long to arrive as the other days."

"I'm counting the hours, Mike."

"I'm counting the minutes, sweetheart. What time can you leave Baltimore? I'll email you the ticket."

"I can get there by twelve-thirty."

"Good. I'll order the ticket for a flight around two-thirty."

"You don't have to do that, Mike. I can—"

"I want to do it, Darlene. Indulge me, please."

"Oh, all right. Kisses."

"Open your mouth, baby, and take me in."

"Are you a masochist? It's bad enough that—"

"Let me in, sweetheart. I need to love you."

"Yes. Oh, yes," she whispered as her breath shortened almost to a pant and her blood raced wildly through her body and settled in her loins.

"There," she said, panting. "You see what you've done?"

"I'm sorry, love. I know what it's like, because I did the same thing to myself. Good night."

"Good night."

"My goodness," Darlene said to herself after she hung up. "Neither Clark nor Tyra offered me any advice about Mike or anything else." She snapped her fingers. "Way to go, lady!"

Mike looked at his watch for the umpteenth time, looked at the arrivals board in the Memphis International Airport and walked a few more paces. The plane was late, and he didn't know whether it left Baltimore late or… He didn't let himself contemplate the alternative. He didn't drink when he had to drive, but he was tempted to break his rule this time. Desperate for some news, he called his precinct and asked Cody if there was any news about airport delays.

"No, man. Nothing's come in here. You expecting someone? Give me the flight number, and I'll call BWI airport." Mike gave it to him. "Okay. Hold on."

Soaking wet from perspiration, Mike loosened his collar and waited for what seemed like an eternity. "If I ever see her again, she's not—"

"The news is good, buddy," Cody said. "Relax. The flight was delayed because of bad weather, including thunderstorms in the Baltimore-Washington area. Expect the plane to be forty-five minutes to an hour late."

Mike let out a long breath of relief. "Thanks, Cody. I appreciate your help. This is… It's a great relief."

"No problem, man. Unless you have one of those airline apps, they don't give you information. Fly on a plane and you give up your right to be treated as a human being. Take care."

"Will do. Thanks again."

He hung up, found a seat facing the arrivals board, sat down and closed his eyes. His body felt as if it had just taken a thorough beating. He told himself to be thankful that Cody hadn't given him bad news, took deep breaths and calmed himself. One thing was certain if he hadn't already known it: Darlene Cunningham was everything to him.

When at long last the public-address system announced the plane's arrival, he headed down to the baggage carousel where they had agreed to meet. After about fifteen minutes, he saw her. She'd probably think him crazy, but he ran to her. He couldn't help it.

"Sweetheart, I've been so anxious. I didn't know what to think," he said as she dropped her bag and went into his open arms. Suddenly, he could feel himself tremble as tremors shot through him.

"What is it, darling? What's wrong?"

"I didn't know what happened to your flight. There was no announcement, no notice of delays. Nothing. I had to call Cody to get information. I was out of my mind." He realized that he was holding her too tight and loosened his hold on her, but only a little. Her hand caressed his face, and then she reached up and kissed him. He didn't dare trust himself to kiss her in that public place.

"We sat in the plane for almost two hours, waiting for the weather to clear. The pilot wouldn't let us use cell phones because of the thunderstorms. But I knew that when I got here, you'd be standing where you said you'd be."

He kissed her then with all the love he had in his heart for her. She parted her lips, took him in and loved him as if there were no tomorrow. He felt a stirring in his loins and remembered where he was. "I'd better get your bag."

After he retrieved her bag, they walked out to the curb.

"I'll get the car. You stay here with your bag. Okay?"

"I want to go with you. I don't mind walking. In fact, after sitting for nearly five hours, I welcome the opportunity to walk."

He looked down at her and could feel a grin crawling over his face. "You are one contentious woman, but, Lord, I love you."

Her arms went around him. "You're bossy, and I don't love that, but I love you."

"All right. Come on." He grabbed the handle of the luggage, took her hand and walked with her to the car.

"We are not going to see Boyd tonight."

"But, Mike, if we stop there on the way to your place, the rest of the weekend is ours."

He thought about that for a few minutes. "You're right. Somehow, we've become important to Boyd, and he'd be hurt if you came here and didn't drop in to see him, if only for a couple of minutes."

Twenty minutes later, they rang Boyd's doorbell. "Darlene, how nice," Boyd said when he opened the door. "You said you'd be here this weekend, and I was hoping you'd come by for a few minutes." He hugged her. "Thanks, Mike, for bringing her to see me. I know you don't have much time together, and I'm grateful for the few minutes you spend with me. Do you have time for a cup of coffee?"

"We'll take time," Mike said. "Darlene's plane was two hours late, and we haven't been home yet."

"And if you went there first, I wouldn't see you,"

Boyd said dryly. "But that's the way it should be. I'll make the coffee according to Mike's recipe."

While they drank the coffee, it occurred to Mike that he had come to regard Boyd as a father figure and a dear friend. "I think it's time you had a meal at my place," he said to Boyd. "What do you say we do that after Darlene goes back? I'm sharing her with you now, but this is it on this trip."

Boyd's laughter floated through the house. "It may surprise you, Mike, but I have not always been old. I know precisely how a young man thinks and what he feels when he's with that special woman."

Darlene told them about the case she'd won. "I'm very excited. Already, my partners are treating me with greater respect."

"Congratulations," Boyd said. "Take it all in your stride. You may discover that while winning that case was important to you, there will soon be far more important things to consider."

It occurred to Darlene that Boyd and Maggie were the only people she allowed to talk to her as her parents might have done. She made a mental note of his words and shoved them aside to be dealt with later.

"I'll call you before I leave," she said to Boyd, standing to let both men know that she was ready to go. She hugged Boyd, and they were soon headed for Mike's apartment.

"Who takes care of this place?" she asked as they entered the exquisitely kept apartment.

"I have a weekly cleaning service and laundry woman. If she could cook, I'd have her full-time. But she can't, and I don't want to trade her for someone who I might not care for."

"She's an excellent housekeeper. Send her to cooking classes."

"I could, but she doesn't really want to cook." He put Darlene's bag in her room. "Do you want to change or freshen up? Tell me if you're tired. I've made some plans for us, but if you're tired, I'll cancel them. I want you to be happy."

"I am happy, Mike. It's when I'm away from you that life gets murky. See you in about half an hour."

She brushed her teeth, combed her hair and slipped on some flat shoes, but she didn't know what Mike planned, and she wasn't going to change her clothes every two hours. When she flipped on the radio, a rueful smile floated over her face. The station was the same as the one she'd tuned in the previous weekend. What would she have thought if someone had changed it? She put her lingerie in a drawer and sat on the edge of the bed, intending to examine what she suspected was a run in her stockings. But she succumbed to a wave of tiredness and fell back across the bed. A pounding on the door awakened her.

"Yeah?" She rolled over and sat up. "Come in."

"You okay? I didn't know you planned to go to sleep," Mike said.

"Neither did I," she said, rubbing her eyes. "What time is it?"

"Seven. I had thought we'd check out Beale Street, get a good meal at Molly's, and dance someplace, if that suits us. As we walk along the street, we can hear the music, go in and dance or just listen, whichever suits you. Do you feel like doing that?"

"I'd love it. I'm as surprised as you are to find myself waking up. I sat down here, realized how tired I was and woke up when you knocked."

With a hand on each of her knees, he leaned forward and loved her mouth. "I was getting anxious. I knocked louder and louder before I could get a rise out of you."

"Well, I'm not sleepy now, so let me get some clothes on. Your plans seem to suggest something dressy leaning toward casual."

"Right on."

"I'll be ready in half an hour or less." His lips moved over her mouth, and when his eyes blazed with desire, she ducked her dead.

"Honey, if we start that, we won't even get dinner."

"You don't know how right you are," he said and hurried out without a backward glance.

Later, as they strolled along crowded Beale street in the direction of Molly's, they met not one but three clowns, each of whom invited them to patronize certain places. One described the food in the place he represented as "bone-suckin', soul-searin' good."

"We ought to go there sometime just to see what that's like," Mike said.

"I'll bet it isn't any better than Porky's," she replied.

"That barbecued shredded pork we had there was so good."

"We can go there tomorrow for lunch, if you like."

She squeezed his fingers. "You've already planned something, and I'd like us to stick with that."

"All right." His smile told her that the comment pleased him.

"Pork rules down here," a waiter at Molly's, who said he was born in Seattle, told them. "If you don't like pork in Memphis, don't order it anyplace else."

"When in Rome, do as the Romans do," Darlene said as she ordered roast loin of pork, grilled mushrooms, string beans and fried okra.

"I'll have the same. Bring us a bottle of white Burgundy, please."

He reached across the table and grasped her hand. "You never wear any kind of jewelry. You have beautiful hands. Don't you like rings?"

She wasn't sure what to make of that question, so she responded truthfully. "I haven't seen a ring that I wanted badly enough to buy. The ones I like carry a heavy price tag. Anyway, I'm more likely to throw away money on shoes than on jewelry."

He stroked her fingers in an absentminded way. "Hands like yours should be adorned."

The waiter brought their food, and she was thankful, for she didn't want to pursue that topic. Should she tell him that she was waiting for him to put a ring on her finger? No way!

"Thanks for choosing this place," she said as they

rose to leave. "The food was delicious, and I enjoyed the waiters' efforts to make us feel as if we were at home."

"That's some good jazz," Mike said as they walked along Beale Street after dinner. "Want to go in?" She nodded. "I hope they're dancing."

They got a table, ordered lemonade and, after watching the dancers for a few minutes, Mike rose and held out his arms to her. "Dance with me, sweetheart, and don't lay it on thick."

"With that saxophonist wailing like Lester Young, honey, don't expect me to be content with the two-step."

"And don't expect to move into me without some consequences."

She brought his head down, tiptoed and kissed his mouth. "Consequences? Won't bother me none."

He missed a step. "Warn me when you plan to do something like that."

"Then it wouldn't be half as much fun. I've been here for, let's see, six hours, and you have only kissed me once."

"Twice. I kissed you at the airport and in your room."

"In my room. You call that a kiss? Honey, that's not the way *you* kiss."

He stopped dancing. "Are you serious, teasing or what?"

He'd asked, so she'd tell him. "Both. This is new

territory for me, Mike, and I'm not handling it too well."

He walked back to the table holding her hand and sat down. "Can you make that crystal clear for me, please?"

Would she be foolish to tell him exactly how she felt at night when she was all alone? No, he didn't need that ammunition. She said, "I need you sometime."

"Look at me, Darlene. Did I get that right? You're telling me—"

"I'm not going to repeat it, so don't grill me," she said, still refusing to look at him.

"Why do you feel ashamed? I'm proud that you need me. I need you so badly that there are times when I can hardly bear it."

She looked at him then. "It sounds terrible, but I'm glad."

He stood, went around to her chair, leaned down and whispered, "Let's go home." His lips brushed her cheek, and she gazed up into the fiery passion exploding in his eyes.

"Yes. Let's go home."

Mike's cell phone rang, but he didn't want to answer it. Then he saw Boyd's phone number and figured that the man had a good reason for calling him. "What's up, friend?"

"I missed my opportunity earlier. Remember that I told you and Darlene last weekend that I wanted to talk with the two of you? I still do."

"We're just leaving Beale Street for home, and I…" He noticed that Darlene's attention was elsewhere. "I don't want to interrupt things just now."

"I see. Can we have breakfast here at about eight-thirty tomorrow morning? Then the day will be yours. I wouldn't ask if it wasn't important."

Mike walked over to Darlene. "Boyd wants us to have breakfast with him tomorrow morning at eight-thirty."

"Fine with me. We promised to spend some more time with him, and I forgot about that. Yes, of course."

"We'll be there, but I'll make the coffee."

"The coffee I made this afternoon was good, wasn't it?"

"It was delicious, but I don't expect you to make that mistake on consecutive days. See you in the morning."

He knew that Boyd wanted Darlene for him, but he couldn't imagine how the man wanted to communicate it. He lifted his right shoulder in a quick shrug, brushing off the thought. He paid the bill, put an arm around her waist and left. Darlene's quiet and uncommunicative mood as he drove them home didn't bother him. Their relationship needed resolution. She had to be aware of that, and it was something that he planned to bring to a head before she left Memphis.

"I'll see you inside the apartment," he said to Darlene, "and then I'll park for the night."

"You'll have to learn, Mike, that although I appreciate your graciousness, I don't want you to get wet while I'm dry or to walk a long distance when you're as tired as I am. Nor do I want to sit in comfort while you park downstairs when I could have the pleasure of being with you."

"All right, but one of these days you're going to lose an argument with me, and it will probably happen over something you least want to lose. I don't give in easily, so don't let yourself believe I do. Another thing. I enjoy seeing to your comfort. It's important to me."

"Okay. I stand corrected. Let's put the car in the garage. You got any good wine?"

"I think I have the same kind that we drank at dinner."

"I'd like some. It's time to unwind," she said, her eyes sparkling with the mischievousness that he loved about her. *Just you wait, lady, just you wait.*

His laughter warmed her. It was so musical, like the sounds of an expert harpist's fingers flying over a great pedal harp. After parking the car, they walked hand in hand into his apartment, and it surprised her that he went directly to the kitchen.

"I've finished driving for today. Would you like white wine or something stronger?"

She lowered her lashes, laid her head to the side and said, "Stronger. But not from a bottle."

He nearly dropped the bottle opener. "What did you say?" She let a long, slow shrug do her talking. "Woman, if I'm not careful, you'll drive me crazy." He threw the bottle opener on the counter, picked her up and carried her to his bed.

"How do you know I don't want to get prettied up?"

"Not now. I don't want to go totally mad. Ah, sweetheart, I love you so."

She parted her lips and took him in. He locked her body to his, twirled his tongue into every crevice of her mouth, exploring every centimeter until, frantic for what she wanted, she captured his tongue and sucked it in, savoring the taste. And when she felt him bulge against her, she grabbed his buttocks and strained herself to him. When he gasped, she tried to climb his body, but he lifted her, and she wrapped her long legs around his hips and pressed herself to his genitals.

All those nights when she'd wanted to feel him inside of her… "Kiss me," she moaned.

"But I'm kissing you, love."

"Then take this thing off me. I want to feel your mouth on me. Unhook this bra."

He yanked up the offending garment, bent his head and sucked her nipple into his mouth. "Yes. I wanted it so badly. I needed you, yes. Put me down and get in me."

"If you don't slow down, honey," he said as he unzipped her dress, "I won't be worth a damn to either of us. I've been ready to pop since I saw you in the airport." He put her on the bed, knelt and pulled off her shoes, hooked his thumbs under her bikini panties and stopped.

"Yes. Take them off. You've got on too many clothes."

He grinned, but she didn't care. She was going to have him, and she meant to do everything to him that she'd been dreaming about. He stripped so fast that she blinked in surprise as he pulled her hips to the edge of the bed, spread her legs and plowed his tongue into her.

She shrieked. "I can't stand it!" Out of control, her hips began to roll as she undulated up to him. He stilled her with his hands and stood to place her lengthwise on the bed. When she saw his huge bulging sex, she reached for him, slid down, slipped him between her lips and sucked vigorously.

"Hold it. Baby, stop it." He jerked away from her, picked her up, placed her where he wanted her, eased into her, bent his head and pulled her left nipple into his mouth. With a finger massaging her clitoris, he began to move in and out in a circular motion. She'd never felt anything like that with him. She thought she'd lose consciousness. It seemed as if he built a fire in her vagina, at the bottom of her feet and in every artery and vein.

"Is it good to you?" he asked her. "Tell me. Tell me you love it, you love me and you don't want any other man."

"I don't," she moaned. "Only you. Help me. I think I'm dying. Make it harder so I can burst, so it will come out. Suck my nipple some more. Oh, I can't stand this."

"Yes, you can. You love it. Give yourself to me."

Suddenly he changed the motion and began to thrust deeply and powerfully, holding her still and letting her feel the man above her. Then she locked her feet around his hips, and he let her move, matching him stroke for stroke. She knew nothing beyond him and the awesome feeling of the orgasm that gripped her body. She felt herself clutch his penis and imprison it until he shouted aloud. "Darlene. Oh, Darlene. You're my life."

"I love you. I love you," she moaned, and then blessed relief as she came slowly back to earth.

Minutes passed, and they said nothing, only held each other tightly. He kissed her eyes, her cheeks and brushed her lips. "We're going to have to do something about this," he whispered. "You're so precious to me."

"All those years," she said, voicing a thought that awed her, "when I didn't know a human being could feel this way…it seems so unfair. If I had never met you, do you think I could have had these feeling with someone else?" She hoped she hadn't made him uneasy, for he was a long time answering.

"I think I understand your question, but I don't know the answer. I've known other women, but I've never felt this way with any woman but you. You're different inside and out. That may answer your question. Are you calculating your options in the event that you and I don't make it?"

Darlene slapped his buttocks. "Trust me. That never entered my mind." She gazed into his beloved face. "But if I lost you, I don't think I'd ever feel this way again.

I'm… It feels so right, so natural. I'm not only happy with you, Mike. I'm content."

"So am I."

He hugged her and fell over on his back, holding her close to his side. She climbed on top of him, gave her imagination full rein, and when she finished with him, he threw his arms wide, panting for breath. Shaken to the pit of his soul.

"If I had to die now," he said when he could breathe evenly, "I couldn't object. I've had it all."

Chapter 9

With one arm around Darlene's waist, Mike rang Boyd Farmer's doorbell, then nuzzled her cheek while he waited for the door to open. He was still strung out from the previous night when she loved him senseless. Her inexperienced fumbling, stroking, kissing and sucking kept him suspended between torture and unbearable pleasure for half an hour. He hadn't known he could feel like that. He kissed her and looked up as the door opened.

"Come on in," Boyd said. "I should have a guilty feeling about getting you out so early, but I don't." He hugged Darlene and patted Mike's shoulder. "As soon as you make the coffee, Mike, we can sit down. I made some popovers, bacon, scrambled eggs, grits and sausage, and you can have cantaloupe or orange juice—both, if you want it."

Boyd had already set the table so Darlene and Mike sat down. Boyd joined them.

"This is wonderful," Darlene said. "I'm surprised that you can cook."

"Of course, I can cook. I wasn't born wealthy, and neither were my parents. I could cook a decent breakfast when I was twelve, and I often did it. How do you like my popovers?"

Mike pulled himself out of his reverie. "They're great. I could make a meal of these, some jam and coffee." He was aware that they talked about trifling things. He and Darlene awaited Boyd's message to them, and Boyd evidently wouldn't speak of it until he'd finished his meal. He approved of that, because he didn't like to discuss important things while he ate.

"I'll clean up, Boyd," Mike said when they finished eating. "You and Darlene make yourselves comfortable."

As if he hadn't said a word, Darlene began clearing the dining-room table, and Boyd rushed to help her. They cleaned the kitchen together, after which Mike took a pot of coffee and three mugs to the living room and put them on the coffee table. Boyd sat down, crossed his knees and drank some coffee.

"I know the two of you plan to spend the day together, so I'll make this as short as possible. I was in on the beginning of your relationship, and I thought that first hour after you met that it would either be short and explosive or long-lasting. The three of us know that I didn't get it quite right. It's still explosive, but you care more deeply for each other each time I see you together, far more deeply this morning than yesterday afternoon.

"Why am I telling you all this? I've been in your shoes, and I can see a crisis coming. I told you earlier that I wasn't born wealthy. We were poor. I worked my way through school, opened a bicycle-repair shop and made enough money to start a business in a field for which I was more suited than repairing bicycles. I signed a contract to do some work for a company, and I fell in love with someone I met there. I will believe until I die that she loved the ground I walked on. We became engaged. Her father died, and her mother was useless for business matters, so she had to take over.

"Well, she suggested that we consolidate our businesses, but hers was so much larger than mine that I figured I'd be swallowed up. Her mother pleaded with me, and Justine—that was her name—pleaded with me, but I wouldn't give in. Since I was here in Memphis and she was in St. Louis, there seemed no way for us to be together. Out of loyalty to her parents, she broke the engagement, but she went into a deep depression almost at once, and no one, including me, could bring her out of it. She eventually passed away.

"Listen to me now. I have wished every day since— and that was thirty-nine years ago—that I hadn't been so stubborn, so pigheaded, that I had seen the benefits for both of us, and that I hadn't been so foolish." He leaned forward. "I ache for her this very minute. I remember like it was yesterday. When I was with her, the sun shone brighter, the sky was bluer and nothing seemed impossible for me. I'm a shell of the man I was then and far less than what I might have been. And I'm not talking about age. I accumulated wealth and prestige, but I don't have a family, not a child, not a rightful heir. I cheated myself."

Mike sat motionless. Dumbfounded. He had come to know Boyd as a kind, friendly man who had a deep need for privacy. Yet, he'd just revealed everything to the two of them. He got up, walked over to Boyd and hunkered down in front of him. "I have never doubted our friendship, but I know now that I'm very important to you, that we both are, and I'll remember everything you said and keep those words with me."

Mike hurt to see the sadness in Boyd's eyes. "I don't think I could care more for my own child. I want you to benefit from what I told you." He looked at Darlene. "And you, too."

"You mean to say you've loved that woman for thirty-nine years?" Darlene asked Boyd.

"Forty, if you count the time that I had her in my life."

She ran over to him and hugged his neck. "I'm so sorry, Boyd. I can't tell you how much."

"Just keep it in mind. Now, you two have a good time. Thank you for coming over."

"Thanks for breakfast," they said in unison.

Mike walked with Darlene to his car, holding her

hand as he did so, but he had a sinking feeling that they had missed something while Boyd told his story.

They went first to the Memphis Rock 'n' Soul Museum, established by the Smithsonian to honor such luminaries as Isaac Hayes, Otis Redding, Elvis Presley, Johnny Cash, B. B. King, Al Green and others of that stature. "I didn't know Johnny Cash sang rock and roll," Darlene said.

"He didn't, but Presley did." They explored all seven galleries, pausing to listen to audios of the famous singers.

"Who was Otis Redding? He had a good voice, but I don't ever remember hearing him before"

"That's probably because he died in 1967, before you were born."

They strolled on, stopping occasionally to gaze at one of the many peculiar phenomenas that characterized the street. A clown who limped because his legs were of uneven lengths stopped them and did a pantomime of a bird in flight.

"Are you lost, lady?"

"No. Why do you ask that?"

"Because you didn't applaud me, and you didn't tip me. That means you don't know you're on Beale Street. I'm working, lady," the clown said.

"I don't know your customs," she said. "Talk to him." She pointed to Mike. "He lives here."

The clown sucked his teeth in disgust. "A local. They don't know talent from ticks." He turned, stopped another couple and began to display his talent again.

"Sorry about that," Mike said. "I don't walk this street much anymore. This is a tourist drag. I don't suggest we spend the day in museums, although this town has enough to keep you busy for a week, but there're a few more that I think are worth a visit."

He took her to the Stax Museum of American Soul Music but, except for Aretha Franklin, he'd never been interested in the artists honored there.

"This place is like an homage to Motown," Darlene said.

"I never thought about that. You're right. Incidentally, I don't think you should skip the Civil Rights Museum," he said, although he'd seen it once and preferred not to see it again.

"All right, I'll go."

They arrived at the Lorraine Motel, and she looked up at the balcony on which a sniper's bullet had ended the life of Dr. Martin Luther King, Junior. She turned to him with tears in her eyes. He put his arms around her, hailed a taxi, and after they got in, she cried on his shoulder.

"It's all right, sweetheart. We won't go in there. Please don't cry." He rocked her as one would a baby until the sobs finally ceased. He couldn't help thinking that something more than sorrow for that fateful April day and for the ancestors she never knew had generated those tears. *Something isn't right. There is no joy, no merriment in her.*

Figuring that what she needed was a different atmosphere, he suggested a picnic along the Mississippi

River. She agreed at once, and he bought a wicker picnic basket from a street vendor and drove to Porky's. They checked the menu and placed their orders. "We'll have two barbecued pulled-pork sandwiches, two orders of warm peach cobbler and a pint of vanilla ice cream in dry ice, two large containers of lemonade and some carrot sticks. Could you please pack it in this basket?"

"Yes, sir," the waitress said. "Won't take but a quick minute."

When Darlene patted his knee, he knew that she sensed his concern and wanted to comfort him. "How do you feel?" he asked her.

"Well, I won't say I'm fine, because I can't lie to you, but I'm getting it together. Not to worry."

As if his touch would banish whatever ailed her, he stroked her back and let out a long breath of relief when she leaned back into his arms and said, "You're exactly what I need."

He drove out Linden to within a block of the river, and they strolled over to the Beale Street Landing, sat on a bench and opened the basket. A gentle breeze seemed to clean the air, and he took a deep, fortifying breath. "Beale Street is so crowded that I thought you could use some fresher air," he said.

She stretched out her legs and bit into a pulled-pork sandwich. "Beale Street is a bit overwhelming for someone coming from Frederick, but I enjoyed it." She pointed to a steamer chugging up the river. "Is that one of those boats that goes back to pre-Civil War days?"

"Yes, it's a paddle wheeler. We call them riverboats. They and the showboats were the trading and passenger boats of that day. I have tickets for a sightseeing, dancing and dinner cruise on a showboat this evening, so maybe we should get back home by three so you can get a nap or just rest."

"Mike, why haven't you ever married? You know why I haven't. The more I'm with you and the better I know you, the more unbelievable it is to me that you're still single. You're everything a woman wants."

"Thanks." He didn't much feel like talking about it, but she had a right to know. "I'm glad to know that you feel that way about me. I've had a few disappointments, one of them very serious. I was beginning to care a lot for her, and she led me to believe that it was mutual. But I discovered that she had an older man who took care of her financially, and she had me because her sugar daddy couldn't satisfy her physically. I had wondered about her fancy clothes, but when she announced that she was spending three weeks in Europe after buying a new Mercedes, I didn't see how she could do so much on her salary.

"I'm a detective, so I did my job. They didn't see me at the airport when they checked in at the first-class counter. I asked the ticket agent for the man's name, explaining that he dropped his gloves and that I wanted to give them to him. She wasn't a quick thinker, and she gave me his name. I discovered that he was rich and married. I confronted her with it and put her out of my life. That was nearly three years ago. When I met you, I definitely was not looking for a woman."

"I'm sorry to hear that, and I'm so sorry that she hurt you. She was a fool, and by now, she knows it."

"Maybe, but I never think about her." He offered her a carrot stick. "I have to have at least one veggie with my lunch and my dinner, and I love raw carrots."

"Me, too. You know, you have a way of clouding my thinking. I've been in Memphis almost twenty-four hours, and I haven't called any member of my family to say I arrived safely. Why do you think that is?"

He hugged her to him. "Because you're happy with me. Let's go. I want you to be well rested so that you can enjoy the evening."

"Next time I come, I'm going to cook dinner for you. I'm not crazy about the kitchen, but I know my way around in one. Besides, I don't want you to think you have to spend the entire weekend entertaining me."

"If I didn't want to show you the city and to take you out, would I invite you to spend the weekend? I would not. Darlene, if you think you are burdensome in any way, then you haven't accepted the way I feel about you. I want to take care of you, to make you happy in every way. When a man loves a woman, it's natural for him to want that."

She gazed up at him, her eyes wide and her expression wary. "It's not easy to believe that I'm so fortunate as to find a man like you. In my work, I encounter so many men and women who don't seem to care if they wreck the lives of others or how many evil things they do.

You… Oh, Mike!" She opened her arms as they stood beside the Mississippi, the sun still high. "You're a part of me. I love you with all my heart."

He picked up the picnic basket with the remains of their lunch, slid his other arm around her and went back to his car. He wouldn't risk kissing her in public. He turned on the ignition and drove away from the curb. "You do something to me. Something powerful. Something that goes beyond the hot stuff. We're good together."

"I know. You bring one surprise after another out of me. Six months ago, I didn't know this Darlene."

"Do you like her?"

"Oh, yes. I love her."

For the time being, that was good enough. He accelerated and, fifteen minutes later, parked in the garage beneath the building in which he lived. Inside his apartment, he said, "I'm going to my room. You go to yours and get some rest. If you don't, the evening won't go as I planned. Something dressy, either long or short, for the evening would be perfect." He kissed her cheek. "See you later."

"Well, that couldn't be plainer," Darlene said as she closed her bedroom door. After tuning the radio to old favorites, she filled the bathtub with warm water, added lavender crystals, stripped and got in. Rubbing her skin with the sponge beside the soap tray, she had an urge to feel Mike's hands roaming over her body, arousing and exciting her.

"All next week, I'll want him and won't be able to have him," she said aloud, "so why can't I..." She stopped herself. "He won't like it if I manipulate him. Tyra would say I'm acting as if I should always have whatever I want when I want it, that I'm being a baby." She took a deep breath. "That's behind you, Darlene, so suck it up and wait till he brings you home tonight."

Later, sprawled in bed, sleep wouldn't come. She called her home to speak with Maggie, but only to help pass the time. "Hi, Maggie. This is Darlene."

"I know who it is. So your plane finally landed."

Darlene decided to have a bit of fun. "It was late. When I got to the baggage section, Mike was so far out of his mind that he literally ran to me."

"That don't mean it took the plane twenty-four hours to get from Baltimore to Memphis, unless maybe you were flying on a Boeing 799."

"Boeing hasn't made any such plane, Maggie."

"That's just the point. In fifteen years they'll make one that can stay in the air indefinitely. I suspect there's no point in asking how things are with you and Mike, since you been so busy, you couldn't call. He ask you to marry him yet?"

She hadn't expected that question. "No. We've only known each other a few months."

"Yes, but from what I saw, a lot of water went under that bridge since you met that man. Remember that if I'm giving you ice cream for free, you ain't gon' volunteer to pay me for it."

"If I'd known you were at your pulpit, I probably

wouldn't have called. Getting married isn't my worry right now. So far, Mike is everything you think he is. See you tomorrow. Oh, yes. Tell my siblings hi." She hung up. Maggie was off the mark. Her problem was what *she'd say* if he did ask her. "I'm a young bird, who's just begun to fly."

She didn't realize that she had dialed Boyd's number until she heard his voice. "Hi. This is Darlene. How are you?"

"I'm fine. I hope you're making the most of the day. It's beautiful out. A perfect autumn afternoon. How's Mike doing?"

"He's in his room resting, and I am, too. He said he's planned a full evening."

"I was going to ask why you weren't resting together, but I don't suppose that's any of my business."

"I'd thought along those lines, but… Well, this was his idea."

"Hmm. Darlene, if you're in love with Mike, be careful. He'll give you the world if he can get it. But be straight with him. You're impetuous, so you'll make mistakes. That tough veneer of his developed from deep pain, but there's still a lot of softness in him, and because he cares, that's what you'll see in him. He loves you, but he won't forgive easily. Keep in touch."

"Thanks, Boyd. I will."

She dialed Mike's cell-phone number. "Hi, hon," she said when he answered. "What time do you want us to leave home?"

"Five-thirty. The boat sails at six-thirty."

"I'm getting excited. I've never been on one of those boats."

"I understand they'll have three bands tonight, country, blues and jazz, and there's a room with an old-fashioned jukebox, sort of like a nightclub. It should be fun."

"As long as you're there."

"You know how to make a man feel ten feet tall and bulletproof. And after what you did to me last night, my feet may never touch the ground."

"If you don't want what's coming to you, you shouldn't be so sweet. See you at five-thirty."

"That's and hour and a half from now."

"Lieutenant Detective Raines, I can tell time. Bye."

"May as well go for broke tonight," she said to herself as she dressed. Her red-silk chiffon left very little to the imagination. Every time he looked down, he'd see her naked breasts. And from beneath her breast to three inches above her knee, the dress fit her like a high-fashion glove. She let her mother's diamond pendant hang in the valley between her breasts and the matching earrings at her ears. Her hair hung below her shoulders, and a few strands fell on the side of her face. Her favorite perfume, black satin sandals and a tiny black satin bag completed her armor. He waited for her at the edge of the foyer, where he could see her when she left her room.

"If I was smart, I'd keep you right here," he said, greeting her with a hug and a grin. "You look exquisite and absolutely tantalizing. It may be cool on the boat—do you have a shawl?"

"Thanks for mentioning it. I'd forgotten." She dashed back and got a black velvet stole. "You look wonderful in a tux," she said when she got back to him, "but you always look great."

She almost felt his pride as they walked up the gangplank and into the *Memphis Showboat*. He didn't move his arm from her waist until he seated her at their table. But he couldn't know that she was at least as proud to be with him, for every woman they passed, no matter her age, gave him a long look. He was the epitome of male energy and authority, and he was hotter than any man had a right to be.

"We'll have drinks here, dance if you like and go to the dining room for a seven-thirty meal."

"I'm in your capable hands. This space is beautiful, and we can see the Memphis skyline from our table."

"This is the bar," he explained. "What would you like to drink?" She told him white wine, and he ordered a vodka comet for himself. Then, he dropped a coin in the jukebox near their table, and Louis Armstrong began to sing "When It's Sleepy Time Down South." He held out his hand, opened his arms, and she was immediately lost in them, as he led them in a slow, sexy two-step.

"I think we'd better stick to the fast tunes," he said with a half smile.

"If we're smart, we'll confine our dancing to country music and Cotton-Eyed Joe."

"We'll do all of it. I want to dance with you to George

Strait's song by that title, to Buddy Guy's "Early in the Morning," and to Duke Ellington's "Satin Doll," country, blues and jazz. I hope you feel rested." She laughed, because his romantic charm put a zing in her steps and a song in her heart.

And so the evening went. She'd never been happier or felt more cherished. On the ride home, she snuggled close to him in the taxi, not wanting more than air between them. At his apartment door, he unlocked it, picked her up, carried her across the threshold and once they were inside let her slither down his body. How could her longing for him have increased with the minutes since she stepped into the tub of bubble bath that afternoon?

She gazed up at him, saw the heat in his eyes and ran the tip of her tongue across her lips. He lifted her to fit him, and when she undulated wildly against him, he picked her up and took her to his bed.

She lay against him, spoon fashion, her naked breast filling his left hand, and his right hand flush between her thighs. Streaks of sunlight filtered between the blinds, reminding him that she would soon leave him. He leaned over and sucked her right nipple into his mouth, guaranteeing him a warm reception. Soon thereafter, she was thrashing beneath him, clutching and stroking his penis. Rending him to helplessness as only she could do.

"Darlene. Darlene, I love you," he cried as he spilled

himself into her. He'd given her all that he had, and she
held him to her as she'd never done before.

"I'm yours. Only yours," she said.

He looked down at her. "Don't go back to Frederick.
Stay here with me. Marry me, and let's build a life
together."

As if he'd poured cold water on her, she sat up and
bounded out of the bed. "Stay here? Are you serious,
Mike? I can't stay. It's never occurred to me."

He sat up and tried to fend off the bolt of lightning
she'd pitched at him. "Let me get this straight. You
know I love you. You say you love me. You make love
to me in a way that guarantees I won't want to be away
from you, and it has never occurred to you that I would
want you to stay here with me, that I'd want you for my
wife?"

She put on his robe, but she didn't sit down. "But you
know I have responsibilities. I'm a professional, and I
have to act like one. It's out of the question."

Mortified, he slid out of bed, showered and dressed.
"I assume you've packed," he said to her from the
hallway. "I'll be ready to leave when you are."

She'd hurt him, and she was sorry, but when he
thought about it seriously, he'd see her side of it. She
dressed, finished packing and telephoned Boyd. "I didn't
realize your plane left so early," Boyd said. She told him
what, in essence, had happened. "He's hurt, but he's a
gentleman, so he'll take me to the airport."

"Hogwash! He'll take you because he loves you. What airline are you flying on?"

She told him.

"I'll be there in an hour."

They drove to the airport in stony silence. Once there, Mike put Darlene's bag on the scales at the ticket counter and looked at her.

"I told you about the major disappointment of my life. It was nothing compared to this. Be seeing you."

A loud gasp escaped her as he turned and walked away. He'd finished it. But how could he? She wanted to call him, but the words stuck in her throat. Her heart seemed to have dropped to the bottom of her belly. She turned to look for a seat and saw Boyd coming toward her.

"He's gone," she said. "He finished it. I thought he'd be mad for a while, and then we'd be like always." She licked a tear from her top lip. "Boyd, he means it. He's through." The tears wet the front of her dress, and she wiped her eyes with the tail of her sweater.

"You said you told him that staying with him, marrying him, had never occurred to you. What kind of a fool do you think he is?"

"I was talking about staying here, not about marrying him."

"You want him to move to Frederick, where he won't have a job? Think it over." He handed her an envelope. "Don't open it until you get home, and guard it very, very carefully. Call me when you get home." He kissed her cheek and left. She put the envelope in her pocketbook. She felt dead on the inside.

How could he have been so blind? She'd worked him over Friday and Saturday nights to make him putty in her hands. Did she think he'd follow her to Frederick like a puppy, live in her big house and let her take care of him? His head felt as if it would split. He got home, made a pot of coffee and sat down to drink it. The phone rang. He hadn't planned to answer it, but he saw Boyd's ID and lifted the receiver.

"Hello, Boyd. What's up?"

"I need to see you right now, Mike."

"Be there in ten minutes."

When he got to Boyd's home, he didn't stop at the living room but went directly to the kitchen, made a pot of coffee and took the pot along with milk and two mugs to the living room. He sat down facing Boyd's favorite chair.

"What's got you so riled up, man?"

"Darlene called me, and I went to see her off. She gave me her side of what happened. I can't—"

"Hold it, Boyd. That woman took me into her body and turned me inside out, reduced me to putty, and minutes later, I have the temerity to ask her to stay with me and to marry me. What does she do? She bounds out of the bed and tells me it has never occurred to her. Don't tell me about Darlene. Damn her. I'm human, and I hurt like hell!"

"Then why was she crying all over me? She wants

to marry you. She just didn't want to remain here this weekend."

"That's not the way it sounded to me. She had time to clarify it, and she didn't."

"After I spilled my guts to the two of you yesterday morning, you're both still acting like blockheads. I saw it coming. She's crazy about you, so use some of your famous charm, for goodness' sake. Don't let that woman out of your life." He handed Mike an envelope. "Whatever you do, don't misplace this. It's very important. Open it when you get home."

"Thanks. I'd better go. This thing is hard to digest."

"You have what it takes to turn this around, and I'm confident that you will," Boyd said to Mike as he turned to leave the room.

Darlene walked into her house, pasted a smile on her face and went to the kitchen to find Maggie. A note attached to the refrigerator told her that Maggie was at a friend's home and supper was on the stove. Greatly relieved at not having to lie about her weekend, she went to her room, began unpacking and saw the envelope that Boyd had given her. She sat on the bed beside a pile of clothing and opened it.

"What? Was he playing games?" He'd said it was important, so she scrutinized it. A puzzle, but she didn't have the right pieces with which to solve it. At the bottom of what appeared to be an architect's draft of a building, she read: "Solve this, and you will receive rewards, both tangible and intangible, beyond your wildest dreams."

She pondered it for over an hour. "The rest of this puzzle has been deliberately misplaced. Never mind—nothing beats me. I intend to solve this riddle."

She spent most of the night looking for a key to the puzzle, but couldn't find one. When she reached her office the next morning, she walked in, closed the door, sat down and telephoned Mike.

"Hi. This is Darlene. I hope you're feeling better than me. Did Boyd give you an envelope containing some kind of architectural drawing?"

"Yes, he did, but I don't have the right pieces. You got one, too?"

So Boyd had a plan for them. *Thank God,* she thought, because she certainly didn't know how to solve their dilemma. "Yes," she said out loud. "I spent the night puzzling over this thing. It can't be solved with what I have here."

"I've just come to the same conclusion. Uh…"

"What is it?" she asked, not bothering to hide her anxiety.

"Can you… I mean, would you come down here next weekend?"

"Earlier than that, if you ask me."

"How earlier? Tuesday, maybe?"

"I'll be there."

"I'll send you an electronic ticket, and I'll meet you at the baggage carousel. Uh…where will you stay?"

"That's up to you."

"All right. We'll see each other Tuesday."

She hung up and telephoned Sam. "I'll be away Tuesday and for the rest of the week," she told him. She was junior, but she was still a partner, not the hired help.

"Be sure and leave your number in case we need to reach you."

Fear gripped her when she saw Mike standing at a post beside the carousel. This was D-day. Would he forgive her? He didn't smile when he saw her. Each bridged the distance between them slowly. She dropped her carry-on bag and held out both of her hands to him. He took them and stepped close to her.

"Did you say you'd never thought of marrying me?"

"No. No, I didn't. I said I hadn't thought of remaining in Memphis, of my living in Memphis, but I hadn't had to think seriously about it. I'm so deeply in love with you, Mike, that I've hardly been able to eat since I left here."

He got her luggage, took her hand and went to his car. He drove into town. "I want you to stay with me. Will you?"

She agreed that she would.

"I know we're not quite back to where we were, but I also know we can make it," he said.

At home, he phoned a restaurant, ordered food and they settled on the dining-room floor with the puzzle. As darkness encroached, Darlene put the last piece in place, and they gazed at their handiwork.

"Do you know what it is?" she asked him.

"I think it's his house. Yeah! Let's go." Securing the eight-by-twelve inch puzzle on a silver tray, he put it on the floor in the back of his car, so as not to disturb the tiny pieces.

"He'll be surprised to see me," Darlene said.

"If he's playing a joke. Do you still love me?" Mike asked.

"Lord, yes. If I hadn't known it before, what I went through Sunday and Monday night would have soldered it to my brain."

"I can't tell you how I felt when I received your call yesterday morning. It was like coming back from the dead. Darlene, don't treat this thing lightly. If you hadn't called me, it would have been over. And, yes, it would've hurt, but I've been hurt before."

"Believe me, you don't have to tell me. I didn't hurt worse than that when I lost both of my parents at the same time."

He parked in front of Boyd's house. Her finger traced his thigh, and he looked at her, first sideways and then fully in the face. She saw his Adam's apple bobbing furiously and opened her arms to him. His resistance lasted for a second, and she was holding him, loving him and sobbing in his arms.

"G…give me a minute to st…straighten up," she whispered. He dried her tears with his handkerchief.

Boyd opened the door before they rang the bell. "I saw you when you parked, but I didn't know Darlene was with you. Come in. Did you solve it?"

"It's a sketch for the design of this house?" Darlene said. "It was terribly complicated, and there was nothing to go by. Who made this puzzle?"

"I did. I could have made it more difficult, but I wanted you to solve it. I own a company of sixty-one employees that makes puzzles and many kinds of crafts. I've retired from actively working there, but I'm still CEO, and I love puzzles of any kind." He observed them closely. "I see you've made up. Wonderful. You don't know how happy I am.

"Sit over here. As you know, I have no children, and no relatives who care about me. Upon my death, my will will state that the two of you inherit this house and all of my property, including my company, Farmer Enterprises. However, to help you avoid such foolishness as Darlene exhibited Sunday morning, there will be a provision stating that the property cannot be sold or divided until ten years after you receive it. If you take good care of it, your children and grandchildren should have a comfortable life."

Later, as they sat in Mike's living room holding each other, he got up suddenly. "Excuse me for a minute." When he came back to her, he knelt before her. "I love you, and I will for as long as I breathe. Will you marry me? I'll be faithful to you, and I'll take the best care that I can of you and our children."

Happiness suffused her as she looked down at him, and love seemed to flood her being. "I'll be proud to be your wife. I love you, and I want the whole world to know that you love me."

He slipped the diamond ring on her finger, and she sucked his bottom lip into her mouth. "You may put my belongings in my room," she said, "but do I have to sleep there?"

"Definitely not." He carried her to his bed and loved her until they were both spent.

Later, they sat up in bed drinking wine and eating cheese and crackers.

"Do couples ever get tired of…uh, making love?"

"Damned if I know. You bet I won't."

"Me, neither," she said. Then she put the glasses on the night table, slid down beneath the covers and caressed him until he groaned with pleasure. "Just a little reminder that I can give as good as I get," she said as he wrapped her in his arms.

On January third of the following year, one month after her marriage to Lieutenant Detective Michael Raines, attorney Darlene Cunningham-Raines opened her law practice in Memphis, Tennessee. As her first client, Boyd Farmer engaged her to represent Farmer Enterprises in a copyright case.

* * * * *

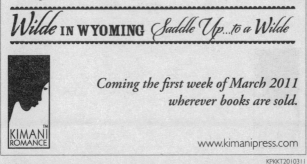

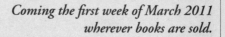
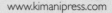

REQUEST YOUR FREE BOOKS!

2 FREE NOVELS
PLUS 2 FREE GIFTS!

KIMANI™
ROMANCE

Love's ultimate destination!

The first in the popular Hinton Brothers series...

ESSENCE BESTSELLING AUTHOR

ADRIANNE BYRD

Marcel Taylor is a ladies' man who lives up to his nickname, Casanova Brown. But he's become bored with it all...until a mysterious seductress enters his world. When Marcel meets "Mayte" at a masquerade ball, he's powerless to resist her charms and desperate to learn her true identity. Beneath the mask, Mayte is hardly a stranger to the infamous Casanova Brown. Yet once revealed, she will finally show him the true face of love.

"Byrd has created a wonderful fairy tale."
—*RT Book Reviews* on *UNFORGETTABLE*

UNFORGETTABLE

Coming the first week of March 2011 wherever books are sold.

ARABESQUE®

www.kimanipress.com

KPAB440031 I

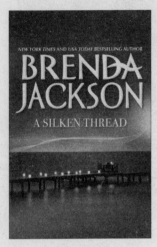